OUTLAW'S REVENGE

When Len Corbett and his gang held up a stage, the passengers were surprised that Corbett then sent the coach on its way — unmolested. Was it the presence of Caleb Brock, or his beautiful fiancée Lucy Lee that prompted Len's behaviour? With the robber gang gunning for him, Len had also made a deadly enemy of Brock, and seemed doomed to hang. But, unexpectedly, he was saved — and given the chance to avenge himself upon those who had destroyed his life.

Books by Conrad G. Holt
in the Linford Western Library:

THE AVENGING RANGER
ARIZONA LAW

CONRAD G. HOLT

OUTLAW'S REVENGE

Complete and Unabridged

LINFORD
Leicester

First published in Great Britain in 2000

First Linford Edition
published 2007

The moral right of the author has been asserted

British Library CIP Data

Holt, Conrad G.
    Outlaw's revenge.—Large print ed.—
Linford western library
1. Western stories
2. Large type books
I. Title
823.9'14 [F]

ISBN 978–1–84617–738–5

Published by
F. A. Thorpe (Publishing)
Anstey, Leicestershire

Set by Words & Graphics Ltd.
Anstey, Leicestershire
Printed and bound in Great Britain by
T. J. International Ltd., Padstow, Cornwall

This book is printed on acid-free paper

1

The six horsemen were motionless, perched high on a rimrock which commanded a view of the valley and the solitary trail below. Back of the men the sky had dissolved into sunset and the cool night wind of the mountains was already stirring.

One of the men, a little apart from the others, was the obvious leader. His eyes watched the trail beneath him, following the narrow white ribbon to the point where it was finally hidden by a spur of rock, and thereafter extended into the desert.

Len Corbett was waiting — waiting as on many a past occasion, for the moment when the overland stage to Ransom's Bend would come in sight. It was due at any moment, towards the close of its long, hot journey from Medicine Point, some 200 miles to the north. There was a consignment of gold on that particular stage for the Ransom's Bend Bank, and Len Corbett meant to have it.

Len Corbett was an outlaw, and the head of a gang of five desperadoes. There had been a time when Len had been a respectable rancher, with a wife and small son. Then outlaws had blasted his homestead during his absence, stolen his cattle and strung up his family. That was five years ago. Len had never forgotten. He lived only to avenge, to find those killers one day. Meantime he had to live, even if it meant stealing gold.

With a jerk he alerted into action. There was a sound in the still air — the jingle of bridle and harness and the all-familiar creaking of a sun-dry vehicle. Quickly Len slipped his neck-cloth up to his eyes and withdrew his right-hand .45 from its holster.

'Ready, fellers?' he asked briefly, and his five comrades — also masked — nodded promptly.

With a dig of his spurs Len sent his horse galloping forward. He continued for a few yards, then raced down a sharp declivity which, by twists and turns, came at last to the valley floor. Here Len took up position in the deep evening shadows and his men ranged out on either side of him to form a solid line. Hardly were they in position before the stage came into sight.

'Right!' Len said briefly. 'Let's go!'

In the natural gloom of the valley in the evening light he had all the advantage he needed. He came along-side the stage, riding hard, his gun aimed directly at the driver.

'Better stop!' Len shouted. 'Make things easier for you!'

The driver was doing just that. The sweating, snorting horses slithered to a standstill and with a crack of brakes the stage became still. For a second or two there was silence, then an angry face poked out of the rear door.

'What the hell's going on here?'

Len glanced. 'Keep your shirt on!

You'll find out soon enough.'

Regardless of the gun, the male passenger clambered out, took a few paces forward, then hesitated as Len raised his weapon slightly.

'No further, mister. My trigger finger might itch.'

The man stopped. It was obvious from his dress that he was some well-to-do cattleman. His face was ugly; his eyes grey.

'I hope you know the penalty for hold-ups,' he said finally.

Len dismounted and walked across to him. The cattleman looked back into a pair of hard, determined blue eyes above the neck-cloth.

'I know the penalties for hold-ups, here or any place else,' Len said coldly. 'Doesn't make any difference. What I want, I take.'

He glanced round towards his colleagues and gave a nod.

'Down with that box!' one of them ordered the driver.

The driver muttered something, then

with the help of his ramrod he heaved the heavy box out of position and sent it tumbling into the dust of the trail.

'Check it!' Len ordered, and almost instantly there was the resounding report of a gun as the metal catch was exploded. Twice more, and the clasp was shattered. Len moved backwards and heeled up the box lid with his boot. A glance satisfied him as to the bags within, each stencilled with *Ransom's Bend Bank*.

'OK,' he nodded. 'Lefty — make sure.'

Lefty, his second-in-command, promptly sliced one of the bags with his jack-knife. What he saw within the bags was quite enough to convince him that it was not sand.

'If you hoodlums have finished maybe we can get on our way!' snapped the individual who looked like a cattleman.

'When I'm good and ready,' Len answered, moving back to him. 'I kinda like that gold fob you've got on your watch chain. Hand it over — and anything else you've got. Money, f'instance.'

The big fellow hesitated, and in that moment Len stared beyond him to yet another figure in the coach — that of a young woman. She rose and climbed out to the trail, her hands slightly raised.

Len did not say anything for the moment. He returned her scornful stare, appraising her. She was pretty, small built, and dressed in a close-fitting jacket and wide skirt. The tiny, saucy hat on her black hair added a touch of piquancy. For the rest, Len noticed that her eyes were very blue and her mouth very determined.

'Perhaps,' the girl said, 'you don't realize who you are attacking. This gentleman is my fiancé — Caleb Brock, one of the biggest cattle owners in Ransom's Bend, as well as being proprietor of the Lazy Gelding gin palace. He's got influence and he'll certainly make you pay for this day's work. As for me — '

'Yes, what *about* you?' Len interrupted, with an odd change of voice. 'What's your name? What's a goodlooking girl like you doing tied up to this hulk?'

Brock glared, but the menacing gun prevented him saying anything.

'The name's Lucy Lee,' the girl answered, shrugging. 'Nothing very fancy about that, is there?'

'Nope. It's not the name; it's — ' Len paused, aware that he could not exactly explain himself.

'Ready, Len?' called one of his men. 'Time we wus gettin' outa here. It's growin' dark.'

'I would no more rob you Miss Lee, than I would my own mother,' Len resumed, still looking at the girl. 'And as for you, Brock, I'm going to let you keep your fob and money . . . ' Len hesitated a moment and then added, 'Put that box of gold back, boys!'

Dead silence. Even Lucy Lee raised her delicate eyebrows.

'Well, what the hell are you waiting for?' Len demanded, with sudden violence. 'You've got ears, haven't you? Do as you're told!'

Lefty nudged his horse forward. 'You gone loco, Len?'

'No! We're just not robbin' this coach, that's all!'

Lefty's eyes darted to Lucy; then suddenly his gun came up at Len. Not a second later it was blasted out of his hand and he flapped his fingers savagely.

'I'm not kiddin',' Len said coldly. 'Put the box back.'

Sullenly the men obeyed. None of them could outshoot Len, and they knew it.

'Now what?' Lefty demanded, when the job was done.

'That's all,' Len shrugged. 'Pick your gun up and we'll blow . . . ' He looked at Lucy and the astonished cattleman. 'On your way,' he said, but his eyes were on the girl. 'There are times when even a hold-up man can change his mind.'

The girl hesitated, then clambered back into the coach. Len waited for Brock to follow her, then he closed the door upon them and looked through the open window.

'Live in Ransom Bend?' he asked.

'I can't see what possible interest it is to you,' the girl answered. 'Matter of fact, I do. I'm Mr Brock's hostess at the moment . . . Anything else?'

'No.' Len eyed her fixedly until her gaze dropped. 'We'll meet again yet.'

'Show your face in Ransom's Bend and I'll run you out of town,' Brock warned.

'On what charge? Don't make me laugh, big mouth!'

With that Len signalled the driver and with a creaking rumble the stage started on its way once more. Len became aware of the gradual closing in of his men around him.

'I'll take charge of this,' Lefty said, his remaining gun in his hand. 'Yuh've got a good bit of explaining to do for this piece of work, Len, and it had better be good.

'Yeah . . . ' Len hardly seemed interested. 'We'll get back to the hide-out, then I'll do all the explaining you want.'

Lefty did not say anything more because he was too puzzled. He watched Len remount his horse, then the entire party galloped away from the trail, up the nearest slope, and so finally through the mountain foothills to the cave which acted as their base. The horses were watered and settled for the night, then Len led the way into the cave and lit the kerosene lamp.

'Time for chow, boys,' he said.

'The chow can wait. You've some explainin' to do.'

It was Lefty who made the observation. He came forward as he spoke, his four comrades fanning out on either side of him. Each stood with a gun drawn.

'About the coach?' Len put the coffee pot down and turned. 'That's simple enough. I decided that we weren't going to rob it. What more d'you want?'

'A darned sight more!' Lefty retorted. 'We planned for weeks to do that hold-up, then you go and queer the whole thing. There's gotta be a good answer fur that, Len! You're just not makin' sense!'

Len was silent. He cast a quick look round the guns.

'Well?' Lefty demanded, coming forward. 'It was that woman, wasn't it? You didn't want her to think you was a hold-up man. That was it, wasn't it?'

Len returned to the coffee pot and swirled the contents round slowly. Then he glanced at the ashes of the dead fire on the floor.

'Better get the fire lit,' he said quietly. 'We're going to need it to heat up the coffee.'

'Damn the fire!' Lefty snapped. 'We've got other things to talk about.'

The coffee pot in his hand, Len moved forward a little.

'Look, there's one thing you mugs will never understand. A woman can look at you in such a way as to make you change all your plans. You'd sooner be dead than become an object of contempt in her eyes — and that's the way it was with me. Therefore — '

'I'm going to kill you, Len!' Lefty interrupted bitterly, but before he could pull the trigger on his gun Len acted with devastating swiftness. The coffee pot flew out of his hand, spilling its contents as it travelled. It was heavy metal and it caught Lefty a glancing blow on the temple. Though by no means forceful enough to knock him out it did cause him to stagger — and completely distracted his intention to fire the gun. By the time he had recovered his balance he saw Len against the further wall, both his own guns at the ready.

'OK,' he said curtly. 'So we can call it the parting of the ways. I could shoot the lot of you down where you stand, but I'm not that kind of a feller.'

Len had been edging to the cave opening as he spoke. The five kept their hands raised, their guns thrown to the floor.

'Never too late to change,' Len said, grinning. 'In spite of what's said about the leopard.' And with that he went backwards through the cave mouth.

'After him!' Lefty snapped, snatching up his gun; then he hesitated as a bullet whanged the rocky entrance way.

'Better not,' one of the other men cautioned. 'He's out there waitin' for us to stick our noses out.'

Lefty breathed hard, fingering his gun.

'Let him go if he wants to,' said Saddles, the oldest man in the bunch. 'Looks like he's two-faced, so why waste bullets and risk your life? We'll be better off without him.'

Lefty was about to comment and then stopped. Suddenly there had come the sound of horse's hooves racing down the mountain trail outside. In a matter of moments they had faded into distance.

'We'll get him,' Lefty vowed. 'He

don't think he can kick back all that gold and get away with it, does he?'

'Right now,' Saddles said, 'I ain't thinkin' about Len or the gold. I'm thinkin' of my belly. Sooner we get some chow the better.'

Lefty half hesitated, then seeing that the men were determined to eat instead of risking their necks chasing after Len he came slowly back from the cave opening and joined them.

Meantime, Len rode hard under the stars, fully prepared for a pursuit which did not come. As he rode he kept thinking of a girl with blue eyes and black hair who had said her name was Lucy Lee. That was enough for him. He wanted to find out now what it was about her that had made him give up the idea of a hold-up. A woman who could do that was phenomenal.

So he rode, presently giving up listening for signs of pursuit. Soon he left the mountain foothills and struck the desert trail which led straight to Ransom's Bend; and a short time after that he was on the edge of the town. Neck-reining the horse he sat gazing, wondering if it was worth his while to venture. Finally, he rode on again.

Ransom's Bend was not unknown to him, with its ramshackle huddle of buildings, tin tabernacle, and the shoddy garishness of the Lazy Gelding gin palace. It was outside here that Len halted and dropped from the saddle. Fastening his horse to the tie rack he strode up the steps and through the batwings.

The reek of tobacco smoke struck him like a blow after the clear night air of the outdoors. For a moment or two he stood surveying the customers, made up of the usual cattle men, cowpokes, and their various womenfolk — and listening to the click of the faro wheels and the gaming tables: then he walked across to the bar, hands latched to his gun-belt in readiness for an instant draw if necessary.

'Rye,' he told the barkeep, and his keen eyes peered intently through the haze for some sign of Lucy Lee. At last he saw her, deep in conversation with a man in a black Stetson. From his appearance he was a cut above the average. His black suit was neat, and the shoestring tie bespoke the professional gambler.

Len only gave him the briefest notice: his eyes were on the girl in her evening gown of black dusted with sequins.

'I reckon I oughta know you.'

Len turned, recognizing the voice immediately. It was no surprise to behold the beefy face of Caleb Brock, his small grey eyes slitted.

'Ought you?' Len asked calmly, taking a sip of his rye.

Brock considered. He was resplendent in a tuxedo, the shirt nearly cracking with starch.

'Yeah, I know you,' he said at last, softly. 'I'd know that pair of eyes anywheres, kerchief or not. You're the guy who held up the coach this evening.'

Len shrugged. 'All I did was hold it

up, and let it go. So what?'

Brock meditated again; then suddenly he seemed to make up his mind. He ordered a drink for himself, another rye for Len, then jerked his head to a deserted corner table. Len followed him, apparently unconcerned, but all his instincts were on the alert.

'I could have you and your boys roped in,' Brock said, when they were seated.

'You'd have to find proof for that, Brock, and you ain't got any. Otherwise I wouldn't have come into town. And I haven't the boys with me. We don't agree on some things.'

'What did you come into town for, anyhow?' Brock asked.

'Just for the ride . . . Look, where's all this getting us?'

'I think, in spite of everything, that you're a man after my own heart.'

Len took a drink, measuring Brock with his eyes.

'I don't know exactly why you changed your mind about that stage hold-up tonight,' Brock resumed. 'Probably fear of the consequences. What matters is that you're an outlaw and have a bunch of boys with you who'll stop at nothing.'

'I don't get the angle,' Len said frankly.

'You will in a minute.' Brock drained his glass and then asked directly, 'How would you and your outfit like to work for me?'

Len was silent. Obviously Brock had jumped to the conclusion that fear of reprisal had caused his about-face in the stage hold-up.

'Work for you?' Len repeated at length. 'What at? Neither me nor my boys would take kindly to a given wage for given work.'

'You're hold-up men — the lot of you. Right. I'm in the same racket as you are, only I don't waste time on stages.'

Len was genuinely astonished. 'You, an outlaw?'

'Let's put it more politely and say

that I'm in the cattle business.' Brock lighted a cigar. 'I've plenty of money. Does that make sense?'

'I guess so,' Len acknowledged. 'Rustling!'

'Yeah.' Brock grinned round his cigar. 'It's bin the work of years to build up a system. Started way back when there were only a few homesteads hereabouts. Everybody blamed everybody else and nobody knew who was really responsible. We took cattle from the Lazy-D, the Bar-16, the Roaring-S, and a number of others. Didn't do it myself, but I had a gang of good boys to help me.'

Len stared fixedly. The Roaring-S had been his own ranch, gathered together through blood, sweat and tears. It had been burned to the ground; his wife and son strung up. It had been a massacre —

Suddenly Len's glass snapped in his hand. He had been clenching it more tightly than he had realized. Surprised, Brock looked at the spilled rye and broken glass splinters.

'Dangerous trick,' he commented. 'You might have cut yourself. Tell Harry you want another one, and have him clean up the mess.'

Len nodded and got to his feet. He was glad of the brief respite in which to collect his thoughts. As he went slowly over to the bar he considered. Plainly, Brock had not been the main person in that massacre, or surely he would have recognized Len? It was only five years ago. Or perhaps he had not known who owned the ranch — yes, that would explain it! Len had been away at the time. He had found only one clue. The rope which had hanged his wife had been tied in a complicated sailor's knot. Few would make a knot like that, and if ever he saw it again Len was determined to hunt down the man who had made it.

He reached the bar and took another rye, giving Harry brief orders. As he came back to the table he was conscious of one dominant thing: Caleb

Brock had as good as admitted *he* had been the instigator of the Roaring-S massacre — and all the others as well.

'What's the answer?' Brock asked, as Len settled again.

Len waited until Harry had cleared the remains of the glass away before he spoke.

'What is there in it for me and my boys? It'd better be good or they won't even listen.'

'Fifty fifty on whatever's realized on the cattle. The brands are changed, of course, but there's absolute privacy as regards that because I have them done in my own corral. Every Wednesday there's a cattle sale over in Medicine Point and that's when I make my deals — the cattle having been sent ahead of me. Matter of fact, Miss Lee and I were coming back from Medicine Point today when you held us up.'

The mention of Lucy Lee stirred something in Len's mind.

'Men have been rubbed out,' Brock went on. 'I'm pretty much depleted.

Most of the men were never much good, anyhow. But I reckon a man like you with a reliable bunch behind him just couldn't miss. There's a helluva lot of spreads around here these days which are just asking to be cleaned up.'

'I'm surprised that you have the gall to tell me all this,' Len said.

'Why not? No witnesses, and you can't prove anything. Are you going to take it on or not? That's all I need to know. It's no more risky than holding-up stages.'

'What are your plans exactly?' Len asked. 'I suppose you've got the spreads lined up in some kind of order?'

'Sure I have, but I ain't tellin' you nothin' until you say if you're coming in with me. You could tip off the homesteaders and that would be just too bad.'

'I could do that even if I agree to come in with you.'

'You could, but you wouldn't want to make things tough for yourself, would you? Only you and your boys will do the job. I shan't be in it at all. Tippin' off the homesteaders would simply make you clay pigeons.'

Len mused for a while and then he slowly nodded. 'OK, I'll take it on.'

'I'll give you the full details tomorrow night, some time,' Brock said, shaking hands. 'Now I've got things to do.'

He rose and went on his way. Len brooded for a time on the turn in events, then raising his head he looked around the saloon and spotted Lucy Lee a few tables away, chatting with a customer. Rising, he strolled across to her.

'Howdy, ma'am,' he greeted her, touching his hat. 'Or mebbe you don't remember me?'

The girl looked puzzled. Her companion eyed her, and then Len.

'Can't say I do,' she responded finally. 'Anything I can do?'

Len shrugged. 'I'd like to buy you a drink and have a chat.'

'And suppose she doesn't want to?' her companion asked. 'She was all set on talking to me. Scram, if you know what's good for you.'

Len raised an eyebrow. 'Let the lady decide for herself, feller.'

The man rose, a tough, thick-shouldered cowpuncher. 'She's paid to talk to customers and not choose for herself! You can — '

'Shut up!' Len interposed quietly, and the cowpoke reddened.

'You tellin' me to shut up? Get out of here or I'll — '

Len's bunched right fist shot out with piston speed. The 'puncher vaguely saw it coming and then the world seemed to explode. He crashed backwards from an uppercut under the jaw, collided with the next table, and finally went down amidst a slither of beer glasses.

'Sorry,' Len apologized. 'You kinda irritated me with your yapping. If I may have the pleasure, Miss Lee?'

The girl, who had been looking on in amazement, got slowly to her feet. She glanced at the struggling, cursing cowpoke.

'All — all right,' she agreed a trifle

nervously; and Len escorted her to a quiet table in a far corner, oblivious to the language floating after him.

'Drink?' Len asked the girl.

'Er — only a soft drink.' She was still looking puzzled.

Len crossed to the bar, ordered rye for himself and a mineral for the girl. Then Caleb Brock drifted towards him.

'I liked the way you poleaxed that critter. You don't pull your punches.'

'No.' Len gave him a direct look. 'No, I don't. And I'm a mite surprised you've no objections to my buying your fiancée a drink.'

'No objections, feller. Just don't go too far.'

Len returned to the table and put the drinks down. Then he pulled off his hat.

'You're too intelligent a girl not to know me,' he said.

She took up her drink. 'Of course I do. I just didn't want to say you're the hold-up man before that customer.'

'So that was it!' Len looked at her. 'I came into town to thank you for what you did for me this evening.'

'Oh? *Did* I do something?'

'You made me and my boys lose something like fifty thousand dollars in gold. That's something, believe me!'

The girl shook her head. 'If you and your boys had been really determined to steal the gold I couldn't have stopped you.'

Len grinned. 'Let's put it another way. You made me see the error of my ways, and I wanted to thank you for it.'

'I'm — I'm glad,' the girl said, hesitating. 'It kind of seemed wrong for a fellow like you to make a living by hold-ups. You're cut out for better things.'

'Just as it appears wrong to me for you to be engaged to Brock. I don't know what type you really like, but I'll swear it's not his.'

'One can't always choose,' the girl sighed. 'There's other things to be considered. Money's the main one, and Caleb's certainly got plenty of that.'

'Yeah.' Len studied his drink again.

'I only met him two years ago. Far as I can make out he originally came frm the Pacific coast, where he had something to do with a fishing fleet.'

Len did not answer. Fishing fleet? Sailor's knot on the rope that had strung up his wife and son?

'Anything wrong?' Lucy asked, and Len gave a start.

'Forget it! Tell me about yourself. Where do you hail from?'

'Oregon. Don't know how I came to drift around here: I just did. I managed to get the job of hostess here and I've stuck ever since. Seems a sort of natural consequence that we should marry.'

'There are plenty of men around other than Brock.'

'True — but not many of them have as much to offer as Caleb . . . And whilst we're about it, what turned a man like you into an outlaw? Surely you're capable of better things than that?'

'I live only for revenge,' Len answered, raising his eyes to meet the girl's. 'I'm searching for one man — the man who murdered my wife and son, burned my ranch to the ground, and stole my cattle.'

'I see — and I'm sorry.' The girl drained a glass that was already dry. Len finished his own drink and sat regarding her.

'You haven't told me your name,' she reminded him.

'Len Corbett.'

With that she rose to her feet. 'Well, Len, all I can do is wish you luck — and I'm sure you'd make a better success of an honest living than outlawry.'

Len nodded and rose to his feet as she turned to go. He picked up his hat, watched her slim form amidst the customers, and then he turned to the batwings. He was on the boardwalk when the noise of approaching horsemen attracted his attention. It took him only a second or two to realize it was Lefty and the boys.

He moved promptly, ignoring his horse at the tie rack. He could get that later. By the time Lefty and the others had dismounted ouside the saloon Len was out of sight.

'We don't know he's in the saloon,' Lefty said, thinking, 'so you'd best stay outside, Saddles, in case he comes back for his cayuse. That's it at the tie rack. Come on, the rest of you.'

They entered the saloon, and of course saw no sign of Len. But they did see Caleb Brock as he came across to them.

'Evening, boys. What's your pleasure?'

'Huh?' Lefty looked stupid, even more so than usual.

'On the house,' Brock explained, leading the way to the bar. 'Just order what you fancy. OK, Harry,' he nodded, to the barkeep.

Glancing at each other in wonder, the five ordered their drinks.

'I suppose you know us?' Lefty asked Brock uncertainly.

'Sure. You're the hold-up men. Don't let it worry you.'

'No?' Lefty looked blanker than ever. 'Well, I reckon that's good hearing even if I don't understand it. Seen Len Corbett around here?'

Brock started. 'Len — *Corbett*, did you say?'

'Yeah. The one who thinks he's boss. The one who ratted on us on the stage hold-up.'

'Corbett . . . ' Brock repeated, frowning; and he was thinking of a time five years previously when the Corbett ranch had been wiped out. He had never seen Corbett himself: he had imagined he had left the country.

'Yes — Corbett,' Lefty said. 'And how come you're giving us a welcome? We expected trouble.'

'Why trouble?' Brock asked, recovering himself. 'Len Corbett's been here, and gone again.'

'Then my hunch was right,' Lefty muttered. 'I sort of figured he'd come here, if only to see that dame Lucy Lee. He's gone sappy about her. But for her the hold-up would have gone through.'

'Do you mean,' Brock asked slowly, 'that because of Lucy Lee, Len Corbett isn't an outlaw any more?'

Lefty shrugged. 'He handed us a spiel about a change of heart and gave us all the slip. We're out to get him for that — and get him we will.'

Brock glanced over the rest of the men and found them nodding in grim deermination. Then his eyes strayed beyond them to Lucy herself. She had come to one of the nearer tables and was intent on a customer.

'Look, boys, there's something I've got to get straight,' Brock resumed. 'I've made a special arrangement with Len Corbett to take on a rustling racket. I'm giving him the details tomorrow night. He said nothing about going straight.'

Lefty took another drink. 'I don't understand it,' he frowned. 'He tells us one thing and tells you another. What was the rustling business you was talkin' about?'

Brock explained the details briefly. Lefty and his boys listened and finally nodded their approval.

'Durned good!' Lefty decided. 'Better racket than holdin'-up stage coaches, but I wish I could feel safe about Len. I don't know whose side he's on.'

'Then you'd better find out,' Brock said. 'If he's stayin' in town there's only one spot where he could go and that's Ma Cranby's rooming-house across the street. If you can't find him come back here tomorrow night and see if he's keeping his appointment.'

'Good enough,' Lefty nodded. 'Let's go, boys, and see what we can dig up.'

He led the way out of the saloon and presently reached Saddles.

'Any sign of Len?' he demanded.

Saddles shrugged, quite undisturbed. 'I ain't seen him, an' his horse is still here.'

'I can see that. I'm told he'll probably doss at Ma Cranby's. Mebbe we'd better go and have words with him.'

'Why? Something on your mind, boys?'

Lefty and his men swung. Len was

only a dozen paces away, one revolver trained in readiness.

'Sorry for the hardware,' he apologized, 'but I don't trust any of you mugs.'

Lefty moved. 'Ain't no need for rough stuff. We just wanta talk.'

'About what?'

'You've made some arrangement with Brock and included us in it. We're kinda puzzled.'

Len put his gun away and moved to his horse.

'Come with me,' he said, and untying his horse, he walked it to a little alleyway between the buildings, the boys following behind.

'OK,' he said. 'So I've made an arrangement with Brock and included you mugs in it. So what?'

'It don't make sense!' Lefty insisted. 'Not after that line you handed us in the hideout. You led us to think yuh'd gone straight.'

'Because I changed my mind about the stage coach? Don't be a bigger fool than you have to, Lefty!'

'Yuh — yuh mean only the stage hold-up was off? Not *everythin'*?'

'Right! Len retorted. 'I've gotta live, haven't I? The stage hold-up was all wrong. There were definite reasons for holding off.'

'Guess I got you wrong,' Lefty said.

'You did — but you can forget it this time. Now, look: this is the layout. Be at the saloon tomorrow night at eight o'clock and get the details. I'm not coming back to the hide-out. I fancy staying in town.'

'Wouldn't be because of Lucy Lee, would it?' Lefty asked.

'None of your business. Get going!'

Lefty obeyed, though it was obvious he was trying to work things out in his own ponderous way. Len waited until the alley emptied of all of his men, save one. It was Saddles, who paused a moment as he turned to his horse.

'You ain't deceivin' me, Len,' he commented.

'What are you talkin' about?' Len snapped.

34

'About you, I reckon. That Lucy Lee means something to you — and I can't see you going through with this rustling racket, either.'

'Leave me be, Saddles. You're smarter than the rest of 'em, and I respect you for it. We'll see how things work out.'

'OK. And remember I'm with you, no matter what.'

With that Saddles mounted his horse, swung its head, and darted after his colleagues. Len made no move for a moment or two then, taking the reins of his horse, he led it back into the main street and fastened it once again to the tie rack. This done, he stood lounging and waiting, watching the men and women coming and going from the saloon.

He moved but little from his position for three solid hours, smoking endless cigarettes and still keeping his attention on the batwings. He saw the last customer come out of the Lazy Gelding, and at length Lucy Lee.

'Howdy, Miss Lee,' Len greeted, as

she came down the steps — and it looked, from the way he was leading his horse, that Len had just arrived and was looking for a tie-up some place.

'You're around late, Mr Corbett,' the girl remarked coolly.

'It's worth it. I wondered if I might see you home.'

'I hardly think so. In any case Caleb usually does that.'

'He doesn't seem to be doing it tonight.'

'Well, no — ' Lucy seemed to think swiftly. 'He's got some work to finish off, and — Come to think of it, you can see me home if you wish, though I can't think what reason you can have.'

Len only grinned and fell into step beside the girl, trailing his horse along behind him.

'Well, what do you want?' she asked, in the same cool manner. 'Get it off your chest if you've something to say. There may not be another chance to see me home. Tonight you happen to be lucky.'

'I've nothing particular to say,' Len answered. 'I only wanted the pleasure of walking with you.'

'What!' The girl stopped in amazement. 'Do you mean there's no *need* for this? That you are doing it just for — for — '

'For pleasure,' Len shrugged. 'And I'll warrant that, deep down, you've no real objection.'

The girl went on again for a moment or two and then she said flatly, 'But I have! And it's not because I'm engaged to Caleb, either.'

Len's expression changed a little. 'Meaning what, Miss Lee? What have you got against me, anyways?'

'Just this. You as good as told me that I'd made you see the error of your ways, yet the next moment I learn that you are willing to help Caleb with a rustling deal. You and your boys, that is. You can't be true to both Caleb Brock *and* me, you know.'

'I'm surprised,' Len said, 'that Brock confides in you to such an extent.'

'He doesn't: I overheard it. Some of your boys were talking to Caleb this evening. It's all quite plain to me. Once an outlaw, always an outlaw. And this is as far as I go.'

The girl had stopped at the gateway of a small house at the end of the street. She paused with her hand on the gate-latch.

'Hope I make things clear,' she said briefly. 'If you've got any ideas about my being interested in you, Mr Corbett, you'd better think again. I've got no time for rustlers.'

'You've time for Caleb Brock, and he's one.'

Lucy hesitated. 'I've time for him because he's plenty of money — no other reason. I've always known by little things he's let slip that he's mixed up in cattle-thieving, but I've had to shut my eyes to it. I can stand it because of his money. In your case there's just the thieving and nothing else — and the fact that you're not as good as your word. The way you talked earlier on tonight I was sure that you'd reformed. I'm glad I know differently. Good night.'

'Good night,' Len muttered, and watched her go into the quiet little house in which she had a room.

2

That night Len slept under the stars. He had no wish for the company of his colleagues, nor on the other hand did he want to go to the trouble of finding a place in town, so he bedded down under the clear night sky, his thoughts mainly with the girl who had decided that the leopard could not change its spots.

With the dawn he was astir again. The desert was still misty and the lingering chill of the night was upon it. Len shivered and drew his mackinaw more closely about him, to discard it again as the molten ball of the sun rose from the uncertainty of sky and the ghosts of the sand turned into clumps of cactus and sage brush. There was the promise of another gruelling day, pitiless here in the open spaces.

Len cooked himself a meagre breakfast from what few provisions he had
with him, drank water instead of coffee,
and then settled himself for the long
wait until evening. As the sun rose
higher he moved in to the shelter of a
giant cactus in the hope that it would
somewhat mitigate the heat for himself
and his horse. The relief was negligible.
Both sweated and chafed at the lack of
activity.

Several times during his enforced
idleness Len debated whether or not he
had been a fool to be thus influenced
by the girl. He asked himself if he had
not been the world's prize idiot to give
back a fortune in gold just because the
girl had somehow affected him emo-
tionally. What good had it done him?
He had lost her in the finish.

'But mebbe not for good,' Len
muttered, staring through narrowed
eyes into the dancing heatwaves. 'I
don't take kindly to failure — even less
where a woman's concerned.'

He relapsed into silence again,

thinking of the job he was to do for Brock. He had no intention of stealing any cattle. He would simply ride with his men and let them do the dirty work. When he had said he was going straight he meant it, but a certain amount of deception was necessary if he was to keep his hand in with Brock.

And whilst Len was thus debating with himself, Caleb Brock was doing a good deal of hard thinking too. Summing things up, he did not altogether like the setup. It still stuck in his mind that Lefty had said Corbett was going straight. Was Lefty wrong or was Len really a turncoat? In such a dangerous job as stealing cattle, Brock had got to be *sure*, and there seemed no way of him being so.

In his stuffy little office back of the saloon he sat brooding, cigar smoke drifting into his eyes. There was another matter too — the name of Corbett. It was not certain that this was the same Corbett who had once owned the Roaring-S, but on the other hand

. . . There lay danger. He was sure of it. Something had got to be done. At the end of fifteen minutes of hard thinking Brock was pretty sure that he had got the answer.

'Might be worth a chance to get Corbett convicted of rustlin',' he mused. 'He's too dangerous a man to be hangin' around.'

Satisfied that he had got the answer to the problem Brock went into action. He tipped off one of his boys, and this individual rode out to the Grey Eagle spread in mid-morning and became engaged in conversation with the rancher. The whole thing looked natural enough.

'Thought I'd best warn yuh,' the 'puncher said, as Bill Maitland stood on the steps and listened. 'I heard it last night in the Lazy Gelding. There's a guy called Len Corbett aimin' to steal your cattle, an' unless I'm dead wrong he'll do it tonight. I'm takin' a risk tellin' yuh this, but if yuh know what's comin' yuh'll be able to deal with it.'

'I sure will,' Maitland acknowledged. 'Thanks for the tip off. Any rustlers who come around here will sure get a hot reception.'

'That ain't all,' the cowpoke added. 'Corbett's the gang leader. The rest of his boys ain't at all anxious to do any thievin'. It's his idea, and they gotta fall in with it. I dunno, but I reckon shootin' Corbett ain't the right answer. Like as not you'll miss him, and then there'll be plenty of trouble later. Anyways, its up to you. I've done what I can.'

'An' I'm mighty grateful,' Maitland responded.

The 'puncher nodded and rode out of the yard. He grinned to himself as he hit the trail for town. Fifteen minutes later he was reporting to Brock.

'OK,' Brock nodded. 'That's just the way I wanted it. I reckon we'll take care of Corbett in a way he doesn't expect.'

And, quite unaware of the machinations against him, Len began to get on the move when the coolness of evening was settling on the desert. It had been the longest, most boring day he had ever known. He was glad of the chance for activity at last.

It was round about eight o'clock when he reached Ransom's Bend, and as usual the activity of the Lazy Gelding was at its height. As he lashed his horse to the tie rack he recognized the mounts which belonged to his colleagues. Evidently they were already there.

They were, seated round a big table in the saloon. Caleb Brock was in the midst of talking to them and he glanced up as Len entered.

'About time you showed up,' he commented. 'I was beginning to think you wasn't coming.'

'I had things to do,' Len responded ambiguously, and dragging out a chair he called across for a rye. Just for a moment he caught a glimpse of Lucy Lee at a distant table. Her head went up in a gesture of contempt and Len compressed his lips.

'Are you ready for the setup?' Brock enquired and, as Len and his boys nodded, Brock went on, 'The first one you take on is the Grey Eagle spread. It's about ten miles from here, due south. You can't miss it if you keep to the trail. Owner of the Grey Eagle is Bill Maitland. He's a tough customer, but you oughta be able to handle him. There's about five hundred head in his corrals and they're not difficult to penetrate. You may have opposition from his outfit, but that's your worry. OK so far?'

'Plain enough,' Len shrugged. 'What else?'

'My own ranch is also on the southward trail — only a matter of three miles or so. You'll pass it on the way to the Grey Eagle. Mine has the name of the Straight-J. Your job is to move the cattle from Maitland's ranch to mine, but you'll have to do it in a wide detour across country so nobody could possibly trace that the cattle are coming to me. Don't ride into my

46

ranch until you've shaken off all signs of pursuit. After you've reached my spread my own boys will take care of everything — changing of brands and all the rest of it.'

'And that's the lot?' Len asked, finishing his rye.

'Not entirely. Later on you'll have the job of driving the cattle across country to Medicine Point, ready for the sales. That means taking them through the mountains by way of Vulture's Pass. The Pass cuts twenty miles off the journey. It's steep and narrow, but that don't make no odds. After that, as I said, it's fifty-fifty on whatever's realized at Medicine Point. Well, that's the lot, boys. Work it out for yourselves and get the job done tonight. If you need ammunition you can get it at the ammo dump next to the livery stable. Be seeing you.'

Brock went on his way to the bar to converse with the customers.

'What do you think there is in this for us, Len?' Lefty asked.

'I dunno, but I reckon it's better than stagecoach hold-ups.'

'That's a matter of opinion,' Lefty said. 'Fur meself I can't figure why you're willing to work fur a guy like Brock instead of workin' for yuhself on stage hold-ups. I suppose there's a reason?'

'Yes, there's a reason,' Len agreed, rising. 'And we'd better be gettin' on our way.'

They went outside, swung to the saddles of their horses, and then hit the trail, riding out of town into the glory of red and yellow which was the sunset.

'You're not saying much tonight, Len,' Saddles commented.

'Nope. Not much to say, I reckon.' And for a time the riding continued in silence. Then Lefty pointed.

'There's the Straight-J!'

The night had almost completely dropped, with its penetrating chill, but the dark was not so intense yet as to prevent the riders seeing Brock's ranch. It was of the usual type, with very extensive corrals. The ranch house itself was low built with a red roof, and there were lights in the windows.

'Brock ain't married,' Len said thoughtfully. 'Wonder why the lights are on? Who's living there?'

'Far as I've heard he's gotta couple of Indians who do the work for him,' Saddles answered.

Gradually the miles were covered. The trail skirted first round the mountain foothills, and then suddenly diverged in two directions. Len pulled to a halt, looking either way in the cold starlight.

'One's the normal trail and the other will be Vulture's Pass,' Saddles said at length. 'Better follow the normal trail, otherwise we'll land in open country.'

They went on again, riding steadily, the night descending completely about them as they went.

'What's the layout?' Lefty asked presently. 'We can't be far from the Grey Eagle by now. We'll have to split, won't we? Half of us to take care of trouble, and the other half to get the cattle out of the corrals. It won't be easy, no matter how we do it.'

'Saddles and me'll take care of what trouble there is,' Len replied. 'The rest of you get the cattle — an' don't forget what Brock said about a detour. Better head east. Saddles and me will see which way you go and follow on.'

'OK,' Lefty grunted, and fell back to ride with the other men. For the rest of the journey no more words were exchanged. Then at length, as they came to the top of a rise in the trail, Len called a halt. Resting on the saddlehorn he surveyed the scene before him.

'Reckon that must be it,' he said. 'Take a good look, fellers, so you'll know what you're getting into.'

The Grey Eagle showed up as a long ranch house with yellow rectangles to mark the windows. The corrals were on the right, faintly visible, and beyond them again was the open country.

'Looks easy,' Lefty said at length. 'We

can drive them into that open country and we've got a clear getaway. That bunkhouse is set well back, which is all to the good. I only hope we haven't got a lot of complicated gates.'

'Let's look,' Len said, and started his horse down the long grassy slope. He stopped again within a hundred yards of the spread and dismounted.

'Hobble the horses here,' he instructed. 'And make it so we can quickly untie them if we have to.'

In complete silence the job was done. Then holding his gun in readiness Len advanced with infinite quietness, making no noise in the soft grass.

'Have a look at the corrals,' he told Lefty. 'Saddles and I will take care of the ranch and bunkhouses.'

Lefty jerked his head to his colleagues and started off. Len remained where he was, surveying.

'Hadn't you better move?' Saddles asked him. 'We're a hell of a way from the ranch house.'

'I know it. This may seem crazy to

you, Saddles, but I ain't having any part in this business. If Lefty and the boys can get the cattle without trouble, all well and good. If they can't, then that's their hard luck. I'm all set for a run out the moment there's trouble. If that sounds like a double-cross I can't help it.'

'I figure you know what you're doing — '

'Drop your guns!'

Len started. In complete silence somebody had come up in the rear of him and Saddles. He half turned his head and could make out a dim figure holding a rifle. He obeyed the order to let his gun drop. At the same moment he became aware of men inside and outside the corrals. Plainly, Lefty and his boys were in trouble too.

The man with the rifle spoke again. 'Which of you is Len Corbett?'

'I am,' Len said, measuring the distance between himself and the horses. He could never make it.

'I kinda thought so — getting your

boys to do all the dirty work while you give the orders, huh? You didn't stage this cattle-steal very well, did you, Corbett?'

'Who said anything about cattle-stealing?'

'Shut up! I know exactly what this is all about, and I'm ready for you. It's as simple as that.'

Len did not answer. He was trying to figure whether this was a deliberate double-cross on the part of Brock, or sheer bad luck.

'Who's this man with you?' Maitland snapped.

'Call me Saddles,' Saddles growled.

'I had a tip-off,' Maitland explained. 'Looks like it was right. Six men don't go walkin' around a spread at night if they've got good intentions. My men are going to take the whole bunch of you right back into Ransom's Bend, the nearest town, and you can tell your story to a judge. You'd better make it convincing.'

With that, Maitland shouted to the

other men grouped at the corral. In response they came forward, forcing the swearing Lefty and his colleagues in front of them.

'OK, boys,' Maitland said, as they came up. 'I've got them covered. Get your horses and ride this bunch of hoodlums back into town.'

There was a general departure to obey the order. One man remained, and under Maitland's instructions Len and his boys were relieved of the remainder of their firearms.

'That's better,' Maitland said. 'And I still don't trust any of you enough to put down this rifle of mine.'

Grim pause. Lefty cast a look at Len, and there was murder in his eyes.

'I have it on pretty good authority that you were the only one who wanted this cattle theft, Corbett,' Maitland continued. 'The rest of the boys only came along because they had to. That right?'

'Sure it's right!' answered Lefty immediately. 'We never wanted any part of it. But Len Corbett's the leader, and so we had to do as he told us.'

'Why, you — '

'Easy!' Maitland interrupted. 'Stay right where you are!'

He gave a glance as his men rode up. They dismounted, and by shoving or prodding with their guns forced Len and his boys to return to their own mounts. Once they were in the saddles their feet were bound securely to the stirrups.

'Just to make sure you don't get away,' Maitland said. 'I'm coming too, to press the charges against you.'

In a matter of five minutes the party had hit the trail for Ransom's Bend. Len, glancing about him in the starlight, saw that there was no possible way of escape. Maitland's men were riding front and rear.

The grim silence continued as the party rode steadily along the trail, to be presently joined by Maitland. It was around midnight when they came at last into the main street of Ransom's

Bend. Even yet, one or two stragglers were about and, although it was empty of customers, the Lazy Gelding's doors were still open and the lights blazing within.

'Untie 'em,' Maitland ordered curtly. 'Then fasten their horses to the hitch rail. I want words with the sheriff.'

He dismounted and strode towards the Lazy Gelding's steps, then he paused as Caleb Brock came into view, followed by Lucy Lee. It wasn't coincidence as far as Brock was concerned: he had been waiting for this moment. But it was in Lucy's case. At the close of her evening's work she was just preparing to depart with Brock. Now she paused at the top of the steps and looked down in astonishment at Len and his boys as they grimly waited for their ankles to be untied.

Catching the girl's eyes, Len looked away. Then Brock boomed a most convincing question.

'What the devil's all this about?'

'Cattle-stealing nipped in the bud,'

Maitland responded. 'Where can I find the sheriff?'

'Sheriff Hoyle was in here not ten minutes ago,' Brock responded. 'Guess he'll have gone home. I'll send Harry for him.'

In a moment Harry appeared and, receiving his orders, went off down the main street.

'Cattle-stealing?' Brock repeated. 'Where? At your spread?'

'Yes. I knew it was coming. And this mug here organized it.'

A thumb jerked briefly towards Len as he stood beside his tethered horse.

'I can't be sure,' Maitland continued, 'but I seem to recognize Corbett now I see him in the light. Ain't he wanted for stage hold-ups? Him and the rest of his boys here?'

'Mebbe so.' Brock rubbed his chin. 'I seem to remember a reward dodger some place with his picture on it. Masked it was, but there's something about the eyes.'

'Suppose you get your facts right

before you start accusing?' Len demanded. 'Right now there's no definite charge — only that Maitland here figured we were aimin' to steal cattle. That doesn't prove anything.'

'It does when you're told beforehand that that was your intention,' Maitland snapped. 'Sooner this kind of thing is stamped out the better. Here's the sheriff now. Reckon he'll know what to do.'

When he came level, the sheriff looked at the gathering in surprise.

'Well, what's the trouble?' he demanded. 'Who's making a charge?'

'Me!' Maitland retorted. 'I want you to take all these six men on a charge of attempted cattle-stealing.'

The sheriff started. 'That's a serious business. Quite sure all six of them were involved?'

'Quite sure! I want the maximum penalty on this one here — Len Corbett, as the ring-leader.'

'It ain't a case of what you want, but of what the judge decides,' the sheriff answered. 'OK, you men — get these six into jail. I'll open it up for you. Then I'll want a few particulars from you, Mr Maitland.'

'Sure!'

The sheriff nodded and went off down the street. Len and his men followed him, and behind them came the boys of Maitland's outfit. Lucy Lee watched the developments and then turned to Brock.

'Ready to go?' she asked.

'Not quite. There's something you've got to do for me, Lucy. I'm going to bring a further charge against Corbett tomorrow morning — that of holding up the stagecoach and trying to take the gold. The bank can prove he tried to do that — the smashed lock on the gold box, for one thing. I'm going to identify Corbett as the man, and I want full verification from you.'

'Isn't it tough enough for him to try and wriggle out of this cattle-stealing charge?'

'Not by any means. He may get away

with that . . . I look to you to support me.'

'Suppose I don't?'

'You'll do as I say, Lucy, because it's your only course. And don't think of walking out of town as the alternative, because that won't get you anywheres.'

★   ★   ★

The sun had been up some little time when Sheriff Hoyle put in an appearance at the small brick jail back of his office. With him were two deputies, each of them bearing a breakfast of sorts on tin plates. They put the plates down on the single hardwood table and then retired to the doorway, hands resting lightly on their guns.

'Get that eaten, and then you're due for trial,' Sheriff Hoyle said. 'Things have bin speeded up a bit and Judge Holbrook's all set to deal with the case. There's other charges against you, Corbett, besides the one of attempted cattle-stealing.'

'For instance?' Len picked up one of the tin trays and started eating the bread from it.

'You'll find out — and so will the rest of you, but as the ring-leader you're taking the brunt of the blame, Corbett.'

Len shrugged and went on chewing. By degrees his companions followed suit; the breakfast — such as it was — was washed down with coffee. This done, Hoyle got on the move. He went at the head of Len and his men and escorted them from the jail, the deputies bringing up the rear.

The journey through the hot street was only a short one, but brief though the distance was to the courthouse it seemed that all the inhabitants of Ransom's Bend had packed themselves into the small space, gazing from the boardwalk rails and passing cryptic comments. Len for his part ignored them. Lefty answered by swearing, until the sheriff stopped him.

'Keep your traps shut, the lot of you!

61

Now get into that courthouse — but quick!'

Len obeyed orders in something of a daze, finding himself jostled and pushed, first by the sheriff and then the deputies, and finally by the men and women filling the courthouse. Eventually he landed on the raised wooden section that served as a prisoner's box, his colleagues on either side of him and the sheriff and deputies watching in the rear.

Len aroused himself to pay attention, and he did not particularly like what he saw. Amongst the spectators on the front row were Caleb Brock, Bill Maitland, the driver and ramrod of the coach that had been held up, and a thin-nosed individual with snaky eyes holding a reward poster with Len's own masked face upon it. A little further away, her face averted, was Lucy Lee. Len wondered what she was looking so self-conscious about, unless it was she didn't wish to meet his eyes.

Len's attention moved to Judge

Holbrook. He loomed over the proceedings like a bird of prey, his thin, acid face dominated by a monstrous hooked nose.

Then, at last, the proceedings began, and the more they progressed the more Len could see how black things were against him.

'I have produced my witnesses and explained the circumstances,' the prosecuting counsel said finally, surveying the jury. 'I would ask you to bear in mind that Corbett is the sole ringleader, both at the holdups and the cattle-stealing. The men with him obeyed his orders because they could do nothing else. Had Corbett not been their leader, there would have been a very different tale. Remember that. On that I rest my case.'

The prosecuting counsel sat down and a stranger rose.

'I will identify myself,' he said. 'I have been asked to defend the prisoner, even though I have had very little opportunity to collect any evidence. In fact I have not even spoken to him. But the law says he must be defended, and that is my task. My name is Lewis Kenyon.'

Thereafter Kenyon did his best, but as Len had suspected from the start, he made little headway. For one thing, even as he had said, he had not the chance to produce any convincing evidence — even granting there was any in Len's favour — and for another the judge was obviously 'squared' in favour of the prosecution. A solid hour of talking did little good, but at least it covered the law as far as a defending counsel was concerned.

'Thank you, Mr Kenyon,' Holbrook said, at the end of the summing up. 'The jury will now retire and consider its verdict and we will — '

'If it please Your Honour,' the foreman said, jumping up, 'we have no need to retire. We are all in agreement and can give our decision now.'

'Very well. Do you find the prisoners guilty or not guilty of the charges?'

'In regard to the ring-leader, Len

Corbett, we find him guilty on all counts, but the men under him appear to have been misled into obeying his orders. We find them not guilty.'

'And that is the decision of you all?'

The assembled men nodded promptly. In the front row, Caleb Brock was grinning widely. Further away, Lucy Lee was staring as though she could not believe her ears. The judge turned and looked at Len.

'You hear the verdict. Is there anything you wish to say before I pass sentence?'

'Just this,' Len said grimly, gripping the rail in front of him. 'This is not a court of law. It's just a rotten pretence of the real thing so it can be said that a trial has been held. Even a trial by the people would have been more genuine than this. You have found me guilty because you intended to right from the start. You haven't even given me time to defend myself — '

'You are found guilty of outlawry and attempted cattle-stealing,' Holbrook interrupted. 'That is all we need to know. The men under you are free to go, nothing having been proved against them. As far as you are concerned, Corbett, the law is that the death sentence shall be carried out — tonight. Take him away.'

Len did not say any more. He was incapable of it. He submitted to being bundled away from the stand and out of the court, whilst his colleagues stepped down and mingled with the crowd in the court, eagerly discussing their good fortune.

Caleb Brock rose to his feet, biting on his cigar. Then he became aware of Lucy Lee beside him.

'What happens now?' she asked, unsmiling.

'Don't look so damned miserable about it Lucy. I've just rid myself of a dangerous man. This is an occasion for celebration.'

'I asked what happens now? I suppose there'll be a hanging?'

'Of course. As mayor of the town it's

my job to supervise it — even supply the rope,' Brock finished, with relish.

The girl turned to go but Brock seized her arm. 'Don't take it so badly, Lucy. Outlaws have to be stamped out.'

'If they'd got the biggest outlaw of the lot it might make sense,' Lucy retorted. 'You ought to be — '

Lucy stopped, stunned for the moment by a stinging slap across the face.

'Take care of your tongue,' Brock warned. 'That's all.'

Lucy stared at him fixedly, sheer hate in her eyes. Then she turned and headed for the door.

'You sure slap your wimmin around,' Lefty grinned, slouching up. 'Still, only way to keep 'em in their place, I reckon . . . The boys and me just wanted to say thanks for gettin' us off.'

'Don't thank me,' Brock replied. 'I didn't do it because I love you: it was because I need men to help me with my own schemes. Corbett's best out of the way. I've a feeling he's playing both sides at once, and that's mighty dangerous.'

'Yeah,' Lefty agreed; then after a brief pause he added, 'Well, I reckon we'll be around town if we're wanted. We don't aim to move out — leastways not 'til Len's bin taken care of.'

'Which, as you heard, will be tonight,' Brock said. 'There's a cedar tree at the end of the street which we use for necktie parties, and it's my job as mayor to supervise. The rest of the details are up to the sheriff. I reckon I'll see you then.'

Lefty nodded, jerked his head to his boys, and ambled off. In a few moments Brock left the courtroom too. Rather to his astonishment, Lucy was on the boardwalk, apparently waiting for him. In some suspicion he crossed to her.

'I thought you'd put me into the dog-house,' he commented, and with something of an effort Lucy smiled.

'Maybe I was a bit hasty,' she admitted. 'I've had time to think. As you say, the best place for an outlaw is at the end of a rope.'

''Bout time you realized it.'

'I'm sorry for what I said,' Lucy went on earnestly. 'I guess I was just that way out.'

Brock put an arm roughly about her shoulders. 'OK, forget it. An' I'm sorry I hit you. I sort of couldn't help it. That mug Corbett gets in my hair.'

Brock began walking in the direction of the Lazy Gelding, and perforce the girl had to go with him since his arm was still about her shoulders.

'What did you mean,' she asked presently, 'by providing the rope for the hanging? Seems a bit queer to me.'

Brock grinned. 'There ain't bin a hanging since you've been in town, has there? It isn't pretty, but it sure is impressive. Everybody in town turns out as a rule. Certainly they will this time to see Corbett swing. The body's left on the end of the rope for half an hour, then the deputies cut it down and take it into the desert. There they bury it, and there isn't even a cross to mark the spot. That's the reward of all hoodlums and gunmen.'

The girl gave a little shiver. 'The ruthlessness of men towards each other! It shocks me, deep down.'

'Shock or otherwise, that's the way it's done.'

They had reached the Lazy Gelding's rear door. Lucy came to a stop.

'No use me coming in, Caleb. I've nothing to rehearse, and I have the afternoon off. I want to know what happens tonight. Do I attend the hanging, or do I — ?'

'You attend the hanging. I shall, and I want you beside me.'

Lucy nodded dubiously. 'Who does the actual hanging? I'm not up on these things.'

'Nobody. Ain't any one person would like to have it on his conscience, I reckon. The prisoner is set astride a horse, usually his own, and the rope is already in position round his neck. That in turn is fastened to the tree branch.

His horse is driven forward and then when the horse keeps going and the rider doesn't it's just too bad for the rider. That satisfy you?' Brock finished grinning.

'And what about the rope? I should think that person can consider himself the executioner.'

'That's usually the mayor's job. Certainly is in my case since the rope was entrusted to me when I took office. I've got it all nice and cosy in my office. You must have seen it on the wall.'

'Yes, I believe I have,' Lucy assented. 'All right, Caleb, I'll see you this evening. I won't say I'll enjoy the proceedings, but at least I'll stand by you.'

'That's my girl,' Brock grinned, and watched her depart along the boardwalk. Then, whistling to himself, he unlocked the side door of the saloon and disappeared within to catch up on some of the morning's business.

But Lucy did not go far. She noted when Brock entered the saloon and after that she crossed the street and looked in the window of the general store, so placed that the reflection in the glass showed her exactly what was happening at the Lazy Gelding . . . and at the moment nothing was.

She made no purchases. She did not intend being diverted from watching the saloon for a single moment. She strolled further in the hot sunlight, mixing with the men and women so that she could not be immediately noticed by Brock when he finally left the saloon. It proved to be a long vigil, an hour and a half to be exact. It was nearly one when at last he emerged from the side door, locked it, and went out to the buckboard he invariably used to ride from his ranch.

Idly surveying the window of the hardware store, Lucy watched him go. When at length the buckboard had vanished from the street she strolled casually in the direction of the Lazy Gelding, glanced once about her, then darted down the side alley where

Brock's office was situated. She had good reason to know the layout, having seen it often enough. Fortunately, the alley just here was entirely deserted and also at this time, as she knew from experience, the saloon was empty of workers. Lunch-time seemed the best moment to put her plan into operation.

As she had expected, the side window was securely locked, but this did not deter her. The skylight ought to be open: it usually was. She glanced about her, beheld nobody, and promptly began to shin up the short gutter pipe that led to the flat lower roof. The havoc to her stockings and the dirt to her skirts she disregarded. As far as she was concerned, it was now or never.

To her delight, her first view of the skylight as she peered over the top of the lower roof showed it to be pushed up on its ratchet bar. That made things quite easy.

She hauled herself over the roof edge, opened the skylight to the full, and quickly climbed through. A short drop, and she landed on the office table. For a moment she stood listening, but no sounds reached her ears.

Satisfied, she went quickly into action. She spotted the hanging rope immediately, halfway up the wall on a peg of its own. Quickly she tugged it down and then took the strong cutting shears from Brock's desk. It took her perhaps thirty seconds to cut rope clean through at the approximate centre. To her satisfaction, the ends of the rope did not fray, even though the five strands showed signs of uncurling. Carefully she replaced the shears exactly as she had found them and searched around for the glue jar.

It was on the nearby shelf. Taking it down, she went to work glueing the rope strands into place. This done she tugged a long pin from her hair and jammed it into both cut ends. Satisfied, she glued the ends together and forced them into firm contact in an exact strand-match. By the time she had finished it was hard to tell that the rope had been cut, and once it was set the glue would make a firm job for normal use — but once pressure was applied the rope would snap like a piece of cotton.

It was not a perfect job, and Lucy knew it. But since nobody would be expecting such a stunt, and since it would also be dark when the rope was used, it was unlikely anybody would find signs of tampering.

A few minutes later Lucy was emerging from the skylight. She put it back in its original position and slid back to the ground. As far as she was concerned, she had made the only move possible.

3

When Lucy ventured out again towards six o'clock it seemed as if the whole township of Ransom's Bend was collected at the end of the street. Some were standing on buckboards; others were pressed four and five deep on the boardwalks. Still others had climbed on the roofs of buildings overlooking the hanging site. Lucy looked at the crowd, gave a little shiver of apprehension, and then made her way to the Lazy Gelding's office door. It was Brock himself who admitted her. She half expected something had happened to give her away, but Brock's attitude was entirely normal.

'I was wondering whether you'd turn up,' he said. 'I've just been signing the papers to make Corbett's execution legal.'

He returned to his desk as he spoke

and Lucy's eyes strayed from him to the rope on its hook. Apparently it had not been touched yet. The glue on it had dried solidly and left no trace. She heaved a little sigh of relief.

'What time does the fun start?' she asked presently, and Brock looked up at her in surprise.

'Fun? So you're treating it like that, are you? Good girl! And the 'fun' begins at sundown — roughly two hours from now. Until then it's just a matter of waiting.'

'Am I permitted a few last words with the condemned man?'

'Under the sheriff's supervision you are, but I can't think what you can want to talk about.'

Lucy shrugged, deliberately not appearing too eager.

'After all, he's going to his death, and as far as I know he has not a friend in the world. In common decency a few words of cheer might help him on.'

Brock reflected and then shrugged. 'All right, I've no objection. Just go to the jail and tell the sheriff what you want to do. He'll look on.'

'I'll go right now,' Lucy said. 'Be back later.'

She left the office, fought her way through the crowds, and eventually found herself at the combined sheriff's office and jail. The sheriff himself looked at her doubtfully.

'Mr Brock has given me permission to say farewell to the prisoner,' Lucy said frankly. 'The rest's up to you.'

For a moment the sheriff hesitated, then he led the way to the back of the building. There were two moderately large cells, and in one of them Len was seated behind the barred door. He looked vaguely surprised as Hoyle unlocked the cell door and ushered the girl in.

'Visitor to see you,' Hoyle said briefly. 'I'll stand here, in accordance with the law.' And he leaned himself against the doorway, watching intently.

Len got to his feet as the girl came to the centre of the cell.

' 'Evening, Miss Lee,' he said, a trifle awkwardly. 'I don't have to tell you that I never expected you coming.'

'I realize that.' Her blue eyes strayed to the sheriff, then back to Len's troubled face. 'As you may know, there's no prison chaplain in a place like this, so Mr Brock suggested I might give you a few final words of comfort.'

'Brock did? That takes some believing!'

'Well, then, let's say I suggested it.' The girl motioned to the bunk and they both sat down so that she was furthest from the sheriff. 'There's not much I can say, except that I'm sorry all this had to happen. I hope you won't think too badly of me for speaking the way I did in court. I was . . . under oath.'

'Scared of what Brock might do to you if you didn't, you mean. I could see through that.'

'All right, have it your own way. I don't want you to go out thinking a lot of bad things about me.' Len became aware of something pressing hard against his thigh. He lowered his hand but did not move his head. He felt the hard outline of a jack-knife. 'Above all things,' the girl continued, 'I hope this will be useful to you . . . these words of mine, I mean.'

Len did not need telling that she was talking about the pen-knife and making words to fit.

'Yeah, I'm sure,' he said solemnly, putting his hand in his pocket, and the jack-knife with it.

'At least,' the girl continued, 'you will be going to a higher type of life. Once you take the final ride out there you will find sudden release. Then you will cut whatever ties you have and find freedom . . . ' She hesitated. 'I'm no good at preaching,' she confessed. 'Sounds ridiculous the way I do it. But you *do* understand, don't you?'

'I think so.' Len looked at her seriously. 'If I don't now I shall later on.'

'Exactly.' Lucy gave a little sigh and got to her feet. 'I guess there's nothing more to say.'

She held out her hand. Len rose, and shook it, looking straight into her eyes. Then the girl turned and went out. The sheriff relocked the door and followed her.

'Satisfied your conscience?' he asked rather dryly, and Lucy nodded and said nothing. She left the jail-office, fought her way through the waiting crowd, then surprisingly found herself near Saddles, Lefty, and several others on the fringe of the crowd.

'Howdy, ma'am,' Saddles greeted, touching his battered hat. 'I'll make a guess and say you've been to see Len.'

'Matter of fact, I have,' Lucy admitted, and made to move on. Saddles fell into step beside her.

'How did he seem?'

'Just the same as any man about to walk to Eternity. Why?'

'Oh, nothin'. Only Len and me are about the only two who understand each other. I sure would like to do something to help him. These other critters are different. They're just waitin' to see him swing.'

The girl hesitated. Somehow there was something about the tubby little outlaw which rang true.

'There may be something you can do,' Lucy said slowly.

'Yeah?' Saddles was instantly eager. 'Like what?'

'You've got a horse?'

'Sure I've got a horse, but what would I want with it right here? Ain't hardly room to stand, never mind bring a cayuse.'

'Something may happen tonight whereby you'll need a horse,' Lucy said ambiguously. 'If you're such a friend of Len Corbett's as you make out, I should have that horse handy.'

Lucy did not say anything more, but went on her way, leaving Saddles staring after her in perplexity.

'Now what the heck does she know that I don't?' he muttered; then he gave a shrug. 'OK — a horse it is!'

Promptly he went and got it from the town's livery stable and then rode back into the crowd. He took up position beside a buckboard, away from his colleagues, and sat with his elbows on the saddlehorn, awaiting events.

Meantime, Lucy had arrived back at Brock's office. She found him in company with the two deputy sheriffs, talking over the final details.

'Well?' he asked, as she came in. 'Did you say your piece?'

'I did my best to give him a bit of comfort,' she responded, at which Brock's lip curled scornfully.

'Comfort! What did he do? Spit in your eye?'

'No.' The girl gave him a direct look. 'He seemed somewhat encouraged by what I said.'

'Did he now? Well, if it pleases you I reckon there's no harm done. Feel like a drink?'

Lucy shook her head and glanced at the hanging rope, still untouched, on the wall.

'I do,' Brock grunted. 'Go through to the bar, fellers, and I'll join you.'

Turning, he took down the rope from its hook and coiled it over his arm. Lucy watched anxiously, fearing every moment he would spot the defect — or else the rope would break apart. Neither disaster happened, for the simple reason that Brock had no reason to suspect the rope had been tampered with.

'I'm fixing the rope in a minute,' Brock said. 'Going to watch, Lucy?'

As she shook her head he strode past her into the bar parlour. She followed into the saloon and sat down moodily at a deserted table. Brock glanced at her once, downed a couple of drinks, then led the way outside. Full of his own importance, accompanied by the two deputies, he strode down the main street, acknowledging the yells of the waiting spectators by waving his arm.

'Bring me a buckboard, somebody!' he ordered.

One was brought up immediately. Brock mounted it, and under his directions it was manoeuvred to the cedar tree. Reaching up, he began to fasten the rope securely to the lowest branch. It took him quite a few minutes, and he tested his own weight on it to make sure — a fraction above the spot where the joint came.

'Reckon there'll be no slip-up in that,' Brock commented, throwing the slack up onto the branch. 'You two deputies stop here and make sure nobody touches the rope. It's getting about time to fetch the prisoner.'

There was a roar of approval from the waiting crowd. Brock jumped down from the buckboard, smiling all over his ugly face — then he started as a stream of nicotine juice narrowly missed him.

'Sorry,' Saddles apologized, chewing steadily. 'I didn't notice you was so close.'

'You did that on purpose!' Brock blazed, striding forward. 'An' get down off that horse! You're blockin' the view!'

'I'm not gettin' off this horse, and I ain't blockin' no view,' Saddles replied, with a glance behind him. 'You wouldn't stop me from having a good look at my old leader's last moments, would you?'

Brock would probably have pursued the argument to a satisfactory conclusion, but there were other things demanding his attention. With a snort of rage he turned aside, waited for the buckboard to be shoved out of the way, and then he pushed through the crowd thronging round the jail. At the closed door he paused and looked about him. Recognizing Lefty he signalled him.

'Yeah?' Lefty asked, coming up promptly.

'Miss Lee's back in the Lazy Gelding,' Brock said. 'Tell her I want her. Do her good to see this hanging.'

'OK,' Lefty grinned, and made off through the crowd.

It took Brock some time to get the sheriff to open the door, he mistaking the hammering for the fists of the impatient crowd. At last it opened slowly and Brock glared.

'Took you long enough! Let's have Corbett!'

Hoyle immediately hurried into the rear regions and unlocked the cell where Len was waiting. Len got to his feet without haste and eyed Brock as he came swaggering in.

'Time's up, Corbett,' Brock announced briefly. 'I've a job to do. Get movin'!'

Len obeyed, still without haste. The sheriff and Brock came up in the rear, each of them with a gun levelled. Then the moment Len appeared at the jail doorway the crowd went mad. Sheriff Hoyle raised a hand.

'Steady, folks! No horseplay! This business has got to be all fair and square. Stand back, the lot of ya!'

After a moment or two Hoyle had his way and a clear path was made from the jail doorway. Only then did he proceed, Len coming after him and Brock in the rear. On every hand were shouts and catcalls, of which Len took no notice.

So, eventually, he came to the cedar tree. The first thing he noticed was Saddles, not so far away, grinning encouragement.

'Reckon yuh've only yourself to thank, Len!' bawled the voice of Lefty.

'Shut up!' Brock shouted, climbing onto the buckboard. 'Let's get this business straight. As mayor of this town I have to proclaim the sentence again. Right here's the prisoner, Len Corbett, and he's convicted of attempted cattle thefts and stage hold-ups. The penalty around here fur that kind of crime is hangin' — '

'Aw, shut up, Brock, and git on with the job.'

'Very well,' Brock snapped. 'You men got Corbett's horse?'

The deputies, standing a few yards away, nodded. Len's horse was in their charge, tossing its head impatiently.

'Right!' Brock said. 'Mount your horse, Corbett!'

Len looked left and right and then moved forward. He knew exactly what was going to happen: he had seen necktie parties before. He began moving but as he did so he manoeuvred his jack-knife from his pocket to the palm of his hand and kept it there, tightly clenched. Without hurry he mounted to the saddle and waited — but not for long.

As he had expected, his arms were seized and bound firmly behind him. Not once did he unclasp the hand containing the knife, and in the now uncertain light the men doing the job of binding him did not trouble to investigate his hands. In a matter of moments they were finished, and Brock came forward. Deliberately he pulled the slack of rope from the branch of the tree and dropped the noose over Len's neck.

'Anything you want to say?' he asked, as the rope hung ready and waiting for Len's ride forward.

Len did not answer. He was staring up at the tree branch. For the first time he noticed the manner in which it had been secured. Definitely a sailor's knot, such as a man of the West would not normally tie. A knot identical to the one which had hung his wife and son.

'Have you anything to say?' Brock repeated. 'It is my duty to ask that. Answer, can't you?'

'Just one question,' Len said slowly. 'Who fastened this rope to the tree?'

Brock frowned and glanced at it. 'I did. Who did you think?'

Len said nothing. He was conscious of the irony. Now he had found the man responsible for the murder of his wife and son he was in no position to do anything about it. At least, not as far as he could see.

'All right, so there's nothing more to be said,' Brock snapped. 'Stand back, the lot of you!'

This time there was no hesitation. Silence dropped. There was a clear track for Len's horse, both for the run up to the tree and for several yards beyond it. Eyes stared fixedly. Lucy Lee turned her head away. Saddles chewed steadily and watched.

'Right!' Brock ordered suddenly, and immediately the deputies slapped the withers of Len's horse. The animal

reared in sudden fright and plunged
forward. Len set his teeth as he saw the
tree coming towards him. In a matter of
seconds he would be in Eternity —

Nearer. He closed his eyes. Then to
his amazement all he felt was a brief tug
and the horse kept on going. He was
still astride its back. He opened his eyes
to find the tree well behind him.

'Hell!' Brock roared. 'The rope's
broken! After him, you mugs — *after
him*!'

It was easier said than done. None of
the men was on their horse, because
they had not expected anything like
this. The only one was Saddles, and he
promptly wheeled and charged through
the crowd. Something close to panic
descended on the remainder as men
dived hither and yon to get their horses,
amongst them Lefty and his boys.

'That rope should never have broken!'
Brock raved, striding over to it. 'Who
the devil's been tampering with it?'

He snatched at the swinging end and
peered at it in the dim light. Then he

started as he felt the stickiness of glue.

'The damned thing's been cut and then stuck together again!' he exclaimed, as the sheriff and his deputies came up beside him. 'How long were you boys away getting Corbett's horse? How long did you leave this rope unguarded?'

'We didn't,' one of the deputies responded. 'Dick went to get the horse whilst I stayed on guard. Nobody interfered.'

Brock breathed hard. He did not know what to say. And meantime Len fled into the twilight with Saddles in hot pursuit. For Len the whole affair was a mystery, but the one obvious fact to him was that he was free. He began to see what Lucy Lee had meant, and he also realized the need for the jack-knife she had given him.

But for being a good horseman he would have been unsaddled by now. As it was, he was one-sided, hanging on by the pressure of his knees into the animal's sides. Meanwhile he worked desperately to unclasp the blade behind him and saw through his ropes.

Dust and sand flew up in to his face as the bolting horse hit the desert trail. The fright it had received in the sudden blow across its withers had not yet subsided. It just tore on and on, regardless of direction, but at least putting an ever increasing distance between Len and Ransom's Bend.

Then, abruptly, things happened. It was just as Len got the blade open and had twisted the knife so as to saw through his cords. The horse stumbled in its headlong flight and dropped to its knees. Inevitably Len was pitched into the sand, the knife flying out of his grip. Shaken, but calmed of the original panic, his horse scrambled up again and stood quivering a few yards away.

Len cursed, his knife somewhere in the grains. He fought to his knees and tugged frantically at his arms, even more desperate as he heard the fast running beat of hooves in pursuit. Naturally he anticipated the worst. All his efforts to break the ropes were useless. Hot and smothered in sand he watched the lone rider come speeding up and his heart sank.

'That sure was some getaway, Len!'

At the voice out of the starlight Len gave a start. He stared hard as a tubby figure waddled over to him.

'Saddles! I didn't recognize you!'

Saddles said nothing immediately. He whipped out his own knife and within seconds Len was free. The bruises he had received in his fall he completely disregarded.

'Better be on our way,' Saddles said urgently. 'The rest of these critters will be along pronto. We can make for the hills and talk later. We'll be as safe there as anywheres.'

Len nodded, whistled his horse, and whirled to the saddle. There followed hard riding and no exchange of conversation. The distant foothills began to appear as a darker line against the night sky. Whatever pursuit there was — and Len didn't doubt but what there was some — was lost in distance. The flying start he had had was the sole reason for his present freedom.

'What the devil happened to that rope?' he asked presently.

Saddles glanced at it, still looped round Len's neck. 'It was the work of Lucy Lee unless I'm very much mistaken. She as good as tipped me off that you'd make a getaway. That was why I was ready on my horse.'

Len pulled the noosed rope from his neck as he rode along. With one hand he inspected it in the starlight.

'Looks like the rope's been cut and then glued,' he said, putting it on the saddlehorn for later inspection. 'Quite an ordinary sort of trick, but it sure worked. Hmm, I'm glad to think that Lucy Lee thinks I'm worth saving.'

'She wouldn't have taken a risk like that if she didn't.'

Meanwhile, back in Ransom's Bend, Brock was still smouldering over the escape of the prisoner. He had despatched every available man to hunt for him, including Lefty and his boys. Now he sat at his desk, the broken rope in front of him. It told him no more than it had already. It had been cut and glued, and that was all there was to it. Scowling, he lighted a cigar — or tried to. The end of the cigar came away badly in shreds, so savagely did he bite it.

He picked up the paper shears to snip the end off properly, and then he paused. His eyes sharpened abruptly as he stared at the shears, the cigar forgotten in his other hand.

'I'll be damned!' he muttered.

There was good reason for his exclamation. Securely wedged in the shears, at the point where the blades were screwed, were hair-thin bits of fibre, unquestionably from a rope. Brock was no detective, but even he could see — when he came to match the shreds with the rope itself — that the fibres were from there and had evidently been trapped in the blades' junction due to their tightness.

'But how? When?' Brock whispered

to himself, bewildered. 'The rope's been on the wall all the time . . . '

He lighted his cigar and set himself to think it out. There was nobody he knew who would go to such lengths to save Len . . . save maybe Lucy. Never could tell with women.

'Surely not . . . ' Brock murmured, amazed — then he paused with his eyes on the floor. He was noticing something he hadn't observed before — a thin haze of white dust and two small bits of plaster. In a moment or two he had figured it out. They had come from the open skylight above, and certainly it was not the wind which had done it. Somebody had climbed through there, and out again.

Brock did not waste any more time. He knew now how the thing had been done. It was simply a matter of discovering the guilty person. And that did not take so long, either. On close examination the flooring of the office revealed faint traces of shoe imprints — dusty prints which had been produced with considerable force, as indeed was to be expected by anybody dropping to the floor from the table, after first coming through the skylight.

'A woman's shoeprints,' Brock mused. 'Guess I don't need to look much further . . . '

He straightened up, tried to keep the anger out of his expression, and opened the office door. Lucy was just crossing the saloon towards the bar.

'Oh, Lucy!'

She turned, then obeyed the call. Coming into the office she closed the door, wondering deep down what was going to happen next. Brock moved behind her and turned the key in the door lock, then he pocketed it.

'Just a few words with you, m'dear,' he said, with that slow quietness that always warned of an approaching storm.

'Sure,' she assented, her eyes straying to the rope on the desk. 'But there are quite a few customers who want me — '

'Never mind that. You seem interested in that rope,' Brock remarked gently.

'Not particularly. Just looking at it.'

'Maybe you'd like a closer look at it?' Brock picked it up, the end dangling. 'You haven't seen it at close quarters, have you?'

And abruptly his white-hot rage spilled over. Lucy staggered back with fire blazing across her shoulders as the rope cut into them. She half fell against the wall as the rope slashed her again. With a cry she flung up an arm to protect her face, and received a stinging lash across her breast, and then her bare shoulder blades.

'That's to start with!' Brock snarled, breathing hard. 'You cheap, low-down little slut! So it was *you* who fixed this rope?'

He threw it down on the desk and seized her arms fiercely, forcing her to look at him.

'I — I didn't!' she gasped, tears of pain and fright in her eyes.

'Yes, you did! I've all the evidence I need. You cut the rope and then patched it up so nobody could tell — not in that bad light anyhow. Why? *Why*?'

Lucy dragged herself free. 'Because I love Len Corbett!'

The words were out before she realized it. Brock stood gazing at her as she breathed hard and looked at him defiantly.

'So you love him, do you? That cheap, no-account outlaw! You silly little fool! Do you imagine for one moment that I'll let you get away with this? You're engaged to *me*!'

'That can soon be altered!' Lucy retorted hotly, and wrenched at the ring on her finger. Despite her struggles, it would not come off.

'Take it easy,' Brock advised, eyeing her. 'If you take that ring off you're letting yourself in for a whole load of trouble. And it's time you were cured of your fantastic notions, too. I'm going to marry you, tomorrow afternoon, and put a stop to this fooling about. In the morning I expect to be busy making a proper job of hanging Len Corbett. He'll be recaptured by then.'

Lucy said nothing, giving up the attempt to dislodge the ring.

'Get out!' Brock told her coldly. 'Get on with your job, and if there are any more stunts like this I'll beat the tar out of you. I was never made a fool of by a woman, and I don't intend to start now!'

Lucy moved to the door and he unlocked it for her. Before she could pass through he seized her shoulders fiercely.

'Walk out before the wedding if you dare! Tomorrow morning I'll give you the money to doll yourself up a bit. Come here about ten-thirty and I'll see you're all right.'

The girl gave a cold glance, shook free of his grip, and went on into the saloon. Brock slammed the door behind her and stood thinking, biting hard on his cigar.

Just about this time Saddles was returning to the mountains. He had left Len in safety in one of the innumerable caves of the foothills, and now he was coming back from an excursion of his own. His saddle-bag was full of provisions, all at Brock's expense. He had also filled two water barrels against emergency, and thus equipped he rode hard and fast towards the mountains. He was completely alone.

After some forty minutes of hard riding Saddles reached his destination in the foothills — a solitary cave on the edge of a precipitous rimrock from which there was a sheer drop of 300 feet. The chance of anybody finding this cave was remote.

Saddles dismounted in the starlight a few yards from the cave mouth and then gave a warbling whistle as a signal. Len's figure appeared dimly in the cave mouth.

'OK, I heard you,' he said, somewhat drily. 'What gives?'

'Plenty, but I'll tell you about it over

some chow. I reckon you must be starving. Unpack my saddle-bags whilst I fix a bedroll blanket over the cave opening. We're taking no chances on stray light.'

Len nodded and set to work. By the time he and Saddles had finished, the food was unpacked, and so too were several other things which Saddles had obtained whilst he had had the chance. An oil lamp glowed brightly within the cave, and a portable kerosene stove was already heating the coffee.

'This lot must have cost a bit,' Len remarked, biting into a crudely made sandwich. 'How the heck did you manage it at this time of night?'

Saddles grinned. 'Simple enough. As you know I returned to town and reported losing track of you. Brock believed me, and so did the other boys when they came back. I said I'd go out and look again if I could have supplies. Brock agreed, told me to order what I wanted and send the bill to him — and here I am. I'm supposed to return and report tomorrow morning. Naturally, I shan't.'

'Thanks.' Len reached out his hand. 'I always figured you were a true friend, and now I'm sure of it.'

'Shucks, it ain't nothing. And let me tell you Brock's mighty sore you haven't bin caught. Search party resumes at sun-up. It might interest you to know that Brock's determined to find you, or else. Come to think of it I could perhaps learn how things are if I ride back into town tonight and question some of the boys. They believe I'm with them in searching for you. Ain't no need to spoil that illusion. Reckon I'll go when I've finished my chow.'

And Saddles kept to his intentions. He took time out for a smoke after he had finished his meal, then he was on his way again into the night. He was away some three hours, time in which Len made himself a rough bed and settled himself for the night. Indeed he was asleep when at last Saddles rerturned.

'Thought you'd been nabbed,' Len murmured sleepily.

'Not me. I contacted the boys and learned a few things. One of them is Brock's found out that Lucy fixed that rope that broke. He's beaten the tar out of her to make her confess. Lefty told me as much.'

'He what?' Len scrambled out of his rough bed and got to his feet. 'The dirty skunk. I'm going right now to — '

'No you're not.' Saddles put out a restraining hand. 'Don't be crazy, Len. You wouldn't stand a chance in town.'

'I wasn't thinking of town. I can go to his ranch. I reckon that's where he'll be at this hour of night.'

'And get yourself rubbed out as sure as eggs. Don't do it, man. There's more to tell yet.'

'Such as?'

Saddles moved into a sitting position. 'Brock's marrying Lucy tomorrow afternoon. I guess he means it. He's keeping the morning free to deal with you, if you can be caught.'

Len took the news in grim silence. It was a long time before he finally spoke.

'Something's definitely got to be done — and something pretty big. Lucy must not marry Brock at any price, not so much because I want her myself but because he'll lead her the devil of a life once he gets her. I still think it might be a good idea to ride out to his spread and shoot him.'

'There's another way,' Saddles said. 'A pretty violent one, but well worth trying.'

'I'm listenin'.' Len settled down again on his crude bed.

'Contrive a stampede through Ransom's Bend at about the time the marriage is to take place. I don't know what sort of a marriage it's going to be when there isn't even a sky pilot in town, but no doubt Brock's got it figured out. Anyways, Brock will have to tackle the stampede with the boys — particularly when they're his own cattle,' Saddles finished with a grin.

Len frowned. 'Let's get this straight.

A stampede of Brock's cattle. How?'

'By lettin' 'em out of the corrals of his own ranch. He's told us where it is, and from what we've seen of 'em the corrals are pretty extensive. Once let out and on the run for Ransom's Bend, nothin' will stop 'em.'

'Maybe, but what about Brock's outfit? They'll make themselves a nuisance, and if possible they'll stop the stampede. It'll be a tough job, Saddles.'

Saddles was unmoved. 'One man alone can do it if he knows what he's up to and has the advantage of surprise. I reckon I'm that man, seein' as you'll be too busy rescuin' Lucy Lee to take much part; My idea is to fire Brock's spread, as far as possible from the corrals. We know Brock won't be there — too busy making arrangements in town. Right! What happens? The whole outfit turns out to fight the fire — and I'll see that it gives them plenty of work to do. When they're in the thick of it, and partially masked by smoke, I'll let the cattle out and get them on the move. Ain't difficult to start a stampede, and the cattle will sure move once they get going. All I need to do is direct them to Ransom's Bend — and with only one main trail that won't be too tough for an old hand like me. Meantime, you'll get to Ransom's Bend and work things out as best you can.'

'It might work at that,' Len agreed, pondering. 'But it is the hell of a risk for you, Saddles. Once one of Brock's boys gets you you're done for.'

'I ain't worryin'. For one thing they'll think the cattle are running away from the fire — and if they think about it at all I'm hoping they'll assume it's one of their own men chasing the cattle.' Saddles shrugged. 'If you've another plan, let's hear it.'

'No, I've no better plan. Go to it, Saddles.'

'OK. I'm going to grab a little shut-eye, then before dawn comes I'm going over to Brock's ranch to make initial preparations. Brock's going to be more than a mite surprised.'

With which Saddles bedded himself down for slumber. It was close on an hour from dawn when he awoke and shook Len into wakefulness.

'I'm off,' he murmured; then he unholstered his left-hand gun and handed it over. 'Take this. It's fully loaded. Just in case you run into trouble.'

'Thanks a lot. Like I said before, you're a true friend.'

Saddles grinned and made his way outside. After a while Len heard the retreating sound of his horse as it departed. Len stayed where he was until sun-up, but his thoughts were busy. Just in case there *was* an attack on this cave, he had better be prepared — and with the coming of the dawn he had a plan.

Leaving the cave, he searched around for — and found — the heaviest boulder in sight. Rolling it back into the cave he tied one end of his saddle rope around it and threw the slack over a jutting rock spur in the cave roof. By dint of much effort he hauled the rock to a height of six feet and there secured it, experimenting. It swung dangerously from side to side of the roof until finally, when lowered a little, it reached the cave opening. In that position it was just as Len wanted it.

Drawing it back from the cave mouth he secured it on the wall. In practice, it meant that once the securing rope was released the rock would swing towards the cave opening with disastrous results to anybody standing there. Outside there was hardly any chance to dodge, with a clean drop into a chasm beyond.

The first one to see the contrivance in the roof was Saddles upon his return from the Brock ranch.

'What the heck's the idea?' he demanded.

Len explained to him, then asked, 'Well, did you do what you hoped?'

'I sure did. I've got Brock's ranch-house loaded underneath with brushwood. It'll fire like a torch when I light it. Good job the building's on props, like the rest of 'em around here. As for the corrals, I looked them over and found the best spot to approach. Believe me, I've got everything sewn up.'

'Good enough,' Len nodded. 'Now have some breakfast. There's plenty of hot coffee in the pot there, on the oil stove.'

Saddles said no more but set to work to feed himself, and afterwards his horse. Then he said, 'The boys'll certainly be on the prod fur you this morning, Len. We'd best take turns to lookout. This afternoon we'll be on our way — you to Ransom's Bend and me to Brock's ranch. I don't know the exact time of the weddin', but I think we'll be all right if we get on the move about two.'

'Fair enough,' Len agreed. 'Now you take a rest. I'll take the first turn to watch outside.'

He went through the cave opening and took up a position against the rock where, from a distance, it was impossible to distinguish him from the all surrounding greyness. From here he gazed into the blazing sunlight across the waste of the desert trail in the direction of Ransom's Bend. The town itself was just below the horizon, but the well-pounded track leading from it was clearly distinguishable. And it was as he watched this track through the wilderness that Len became aware of certain movement.

First it was apparent as a cloud of dust wisping into the hot sky, then it lightened somewhat and specks were visible darting off in various directions. Obviously the search party was on the move.

4

For an hour and more Len watched the comings and goings, at which time Saddles came out to take his turn of duty. He watched the men through narrowed eyes, and then spat casually.

'Leastways you know where they are,' he said. 'You'll have to make a long detour into town.'

'I reckon so.' Len turned towards the cave opening. 'Guess I'll try an' get a shave. There's a broken bottle that might be useful.'

Saddles said nothing. He rolled a cigarette for himself and took up his position as sentry, complacently surveying the activities of the search party far away.

And in Ransom's Bend itself Brock had all his arrangements complete. Because of his importance in the town, nothing less than the church would do for his wedding. All morning his men were hard at work, clearing it for action. Whilst they were doing this he had his lawyer draw up a special licence, which in his capacity as Registrar of Ransom's Bend it was in his province to do. Then an early telegraph call to a minister at Medicine Point completed the business. By three o'clock the reverend gentleman ought to have arrived. He had been warned by Brock some time before that his services might be needed in a hurry, and that moment had come.

The least interested in the proceedings was Lucy Lee herself. Though she had absolute *carte blanche* from Brock to buy whatever she needed for her wedding regalia, she went about it in a completely dispirited fashion. Towards two o'clock two very over-dressed, over-perfumed ladies presented themselves and Lucy was forced to accept their company as bridesmaids. She had strong suspicions they were actually scrub women from the gin palace.

So, for the unsmiling Lucy, the

ghastly farce of preparation went on. She thought once of breaking free and making a dash for it, but since that would probably have earned her a bullet in the back she decided against it. While she was alive she could still fight.

Brock's best man was the foreman of his ranch, Ted Realing, whose knowledge of the functions of a best man was about zero. The same could be said about the barkeep who was to give the bride away. Towards two o'clock Brock was commencing to have last-minute nerves.

They were not improved by the return of Lefty and the rest of the search party. Brock, just emerging from Joe's Hash House after a hasty lunch, scowled as he saw the riders loping into town.

'This the best y'can do?' he demanded, as Lefty rode up to him. 'Where's Corbett?'

'We just don't know,' Lefty shrugged. 'We've bin searchin' all morning, the whole lot of us — except Saddles, who seems to have vanished somewhere

— an' we can't find Corbett.'

'Naturally, with Saddles on his side!' Brock snapped. 'Saddles has pulled a fast one: I'm sure of it by now. He's tipped off Corbett what we're doing. We'll be lucky if we ever find him.'

There was an uncomfortable silence for a moment, then Lefty said, 'I reckon we could start a search of the foothills, but it might take weeks. You know what the foothills are.'

'Yeah, I know — and know too what a lot of damned bunglers you fellers are. You'd better begin a systematic search, starting tomorrow. I'll need you this afternoon to cheer up the wedding. Get yourselves cleaned up a bit. There ain't overmuch time.'

Lefty jerked his head to the rest of the men, then swung his horse's head and trailed off.

And, in the mountain foothills, events were moving. Len had seen the departure of the search party for Ransom's Bend, and when he had judged the way was clear he had started off with his single gun to carry out his part of the programme. Not so long after him came Saddles, riding swiftly in a wide detour to Brock's ranch.

He approached it from the east, thereby attracting the least attention, towards half past two. He took the risk of riding to within 500 yards and there hobbled his horse. From this position he faced the back of the ranch house where there were no windows, and anybody in the yards or barns would not see him because of the bulk of the ranch house itself.

'So far, so good,' he muttered, glancing about him; then he made a sudden dive forward and ended up on his knees, peering at the preparations he had made under the ranch house. As he had expected, everything was as he had left it. Nothing had been disturbed.

It was only a moment's work for him to fire the hay. It flared into instant flame, so much so that he had to beat a hurried retreat — but not a disordered one. He knew exactly what he was doing and retired behind a nearby barn to watch results. They were not long in coming. Frantic shouting merged into hurrying men.

By this time the blaze was a furious one. There was just nothing to stop it. In a matter of minutes Brock's home was blazing merrily and pouring forth clouds of dense, choking smoke. It did not drift much since there was no wind, but it certainly produced a murky pall over the yards and corrals.

Saddles chuckled to himself and moved fast in the direction of the corrals, the smoke providing complete cover. He caught glimpses of frantic cowpokes busy with a human chain of water buckets; he heard the shouts of panic.

Saddles' next actions called for a good deal of nerve and precision. He unfastened the gates of the corral and, with his long experience of cattle, he very soon got the beasts on the move, driving them away from the ranch in a continuous stream. When he was satisfied that they would pursue a follow-my-leader act he dodged round the holocaust which was the ranch, quite unnoticed by the desperately working men, and reached his horse.

After that the situation was easier for him. By this time the cattle had broken well clear of the corrals and were moving in complete disorder, but instinctively away from the fire. Then Saddles came up behind them and with shouts and whip succeeded in dragooning them into a packed mass. Here again the luck held for there was so much noise going on at the blazing ranch, the fire having now leapt to barns and out-houses, that his own shouts were not even noticed.

Once he felt it was safe to do so, Saddles resorted to his gun, and this indeed brought panic to the already startled herd. The fire, gunshots, and occasional slashes of the whip, were enough to break down their last reserves and plunge them into a real stampede. Saddles grinned in satisfaction as he saw the beasts were blundering along the desert trail, exactly as he had hoped they would. Nothing could now stop them arriving in Ransom's Bend, and then indeed there would be fun in plenty.

Meantime, an unobserved watcher was idling on the roof of the town's tabernacle. Nearby, tied in such a way to make a quick departure immediately possible, was his horse. One horse amidst so many did not mean a thing since the town's populace was turning out to see the wedding.

The watcher was Len Corbett. It had seemed to him after his cautious approach to the town from the rear that the best possible vantage point was on the roof where he could stay hidden by the cockeyed little steeple. Further, there were skylights in the roof, several of them pushed partly open to relieve the scorching heat — so he could observe the interior proceedings as well. Added to this he had a view of the desert trail, and if Saddles' plan succeeded he hoped before long to get some glimpse of the stampeding cattle. If he did not, then things were going to be difficult indeed. But since he had come this far without detection Len meant to finish the job of stopping Lucy marrying Brock, even if it cost him his life.

At the moment things were just commencing to take shape. The folks of Ransom's Bend were congregated on either side of the main street, most of them on the boardwalks but one or two getting a grandstand seat from buckboard or horse. Amongst the spectators nearer the church Len was quick to see Lefty and the two deputy sheriffs. It made him grin cynically. So near to their quarry, yet completely unaware of it!

It was towards 2.30 when things really began to happen. Brock appeared from the vicinity of his office and walked with a considerable swagger down the clear stretch in the centre of the street, acknowledging the cheers — somewhat ironical — with a raised hand. He marched on steadily and into the church, after which several of his cohorts, dressed for the occasion, followed suit. It seemed to be the signal for the general public to get on the move, and they began crowding swiftly into the church.

Len transferred his attention to a skylight. He could see the clergyman from Medicine Point standing on the raised dais, and one or two spectators on the front row. Beyond that, his view was limited, but the general indications were that it would not be long now.

Anxiously Len raised his eyes and scanned the desert trail. Nothing happening so far. If it did not come soon he would have to take desperate chances . . . then a further outburst of cheering brought his attention back to the main street.

Lucy Lee had arrived! And in spite of her sullen expression she looked quite delectable. Then there came a sound, different from the general noise of the crowd, as the girl reached the church steps. Len was the first to hear it in his isolated position, and he turned quickly. At what he saw he drew a deep breath. There was a haze of dust on the desert trail, accompanied by the lowing and blatting of disturbed cattle.

Those below had not yet realized what was happening. Lucy went into the church, followed by her brides-maids. Len snatched his gun from his belt and stood by the skylight, ready for action. The din of approaching cattle came nearer, so much so that one or two people looked out towards the desert.

Len breathed hard. Why the devil didn't the cattle hurry up? This perhaps was a pointless question for the cattle were moving fast — very fast — com-pletely stampeded by this time, and Saddles was in the rear to see that they stayed that way.

Len looked back below. Brock and Lucy were kneeling side by side and the minister was uttering the first lines of the marriage ceremony — then it dawned upon somebody outside that there was real trouble coming in from the desert.

'It's cattle!'

'A stampede heading this way!'

'Get out — quick — '

Those within the church could not fail to hear the shouts. Even more, they could hear the thunderous rumble as the maddened beasts came nearer. The minister raised his head in puzzlement and Brock glanced behind him. Suddenly there was a stirring amidst the spectators.

'Stampede, Mr Brock!' bawled a man in the church doorway.

'Stampede?' Brock got to his feet. 'It just isn't possible — '

'I can hear them,' Lucy interrupted, also rising and looking about her.

For a second or two there was hesitation. Everybody knew what a stampede meant — the blind, senseless onrush of cattle with their heavy bodies and blundering feet. Ransom's Bend, with its matchwood buildings, would undoubtedly take a battering.

The hesitation did not last long. The people began moving — and fast, not only those in the church, but in the main street as well. Hardly had they got a short distance, however, before the first cattle arrived, to instantly thicken as more poured up behind them. Those which could force their way up the main street turned sideways, crashing into shop windows, battering down doors, and even stumbling up the steps of the church.

'Those are *my* steers!' came a sudden yell from Brock. 'They've got my brand on 'em! What the hell's going on?'

The wedding completely forgotten, Brock pushed through the midst of the scared men and women trying to make an exit. Lucy was left standing, undecided what to do, which was the one chance Len was waiting for.

Regardless of the danger he whipped the nearby skylight wide open and signalled the girl quickly. She looked up, gave a start of surprise, and then looked back at Brock as he managed to force a way to the front doors. There he stood gazing in speechless fury on his own cattle surging through the main street.

'Jump!' Len insisted, as Lucy looked at him again. 'Jump up! It's your last chance to get away!'

Nobody heard him amidst the noise, and the minister had long since fled into the crowd. Isolated as she was Lucy had the supreme chance. She suddenly made up her mind, stretched her hands to the limit overhead, and leapt. Len was ready for her. He gripped her wrists tightly and, bracing himself hauled her slowly upwards.

Finally gripping her beneath the armpits he heaved with all his strength, but tearing her wedding dress disastrously in the process. Brock, turning from the doorway, was just in time to see a pair of shapely legs vanishing through the roof — and even now he did not suspect the truth. He imagined the girl was escaping the stampede that way. He had too much on his mind to question how she had even managed to leap so high unaided.

A last pull and Lucy was planted firmly on the roof. She stood up beside Len and the ghost of a smile crossed her face.

'Willing to take a chance with me?' he questioned.

'Sure thing! I've taken plenty already, haven't I?'

Len waited no longer. His gun in one hand, and his other arm about the girl's waist, he moved to the edge of the roof. His horse was still where he had left it at the back of the church. To the front the cattle rush was thinning, but clouds of dust and shouting men and women were everywhere.

'We'll go down the way I came up,' Len decided, and promptly leapt over the low parapet to the next lower roof of the church; then he held up his hands to catch the girl. She followed after him swiftly, after deliberately tearing her wedding dress skirt to the knees to allow more liberty.

'Down the gutter pipe,' Len said, and suited the action to the word — again catching Lucy as she dropped. Then together they raced across to his horse.

'Quick!' he said urgently, and whirled her to the saddle.

The moment she was seated, albeit uncomfortably, Len whipped the reins into their normal position and vaulted up beside her. A few words to the horse, a dig from his spurs, and the animal was on its way, going hell-for-leather for the desert trail. Almost instantly there came the sound of pursuing hoofbeats.

'Take it easy!' bawled Saddles' voice. 'I don't want to kick off just yet!'

Grinning, his face streaked in sweat and dirt, he rode level. Not for an instant was speed slackened. Everything depended on putting as big a distance as possible between themselves and Ransom's Bend.

'So you made it, then?' Saddles went on, somewhat breathlessly. 'Nice work! Howdy, Miss Lee.'

'Howdy yourself,' she responded promptly. 'I certainly didn't expect anything like this when I started off for the wedding.'

'Neither did Brock,' Len grinned. 'I don't think he's found out yet that you've vanished. When he does he'll be quite peevish.'

Saddles glanced rearward. 'No sign of pursuit, anyway. I reckon they'll have their hands full bringing that stampede to a stop. Me? I just drove the brutes as far as the main street and then retreated to watch what happened. Caught sight of you two, and there it is. Brock's sure got plenty of grief on his head, especially with the burning down of his ranch.'

Right at that moment Caleb Brock was cursing a good deal. With the sheriff and his deputies, Lefty and his boys, and one or two others, he was still in the midst of getting order out of chaos, and being still attired in the splendour of his wedding outfit he cut a rather incongruous figure — but at least he knew how to handle the situation. By degrees, under his direction, the cattle were turned off into a field at the bottom end of the main street and once there they gradually calmed. Then, and then only, did a somewhat dazed populace begin to assess the damage.

Not that the damage worried Brock particularly. Another matter was turning him livid with fury.

'Who the hell did this?' he demanded of the sheriff. 'Who?'

'I know no more 'n you, Mr Brock.'

Brock jerked his dusty jacket into place and flattened his hair.

'Let's get back to the ceremony . . . that is if that blasted minister hasn't taken fright.'

Apparently the minister was not the only one who had deserted. A goodly proportion of the spectators had gone, including the best man, and above all Lucy herself.

'What *is* this?' Brock roared, glaring round. 'Where's the foreman? Where's Lucy Lee?'

At that moment the foreman himself came up. 'One of the boys just rode in from your spread, Mr Brock. Afraid I've got bad news. Your ranch house has been burned to the ground. It was that fire that caused the cattle stampede . . .'

Brock stood perfectly still, his colour changing. Finally he exploded.

'Corbett! Corbett, the dirty skunk! And Saddles too maybe.'

'Looks that way. I'd better get back to the spread — '

'Don't be an idiot! There's nothing you can do with a burned-out spread. Get some of the boys and get the cattle back to the corrals. Right now there's the wedding . . . where's Lucy?'

The assembly looked at each other and shrugged.

'I don't know where she is,' the foreman said. 'And anyways, the parson has vamoosed.'

Brock clenched his fists and looked around him with homicidal fury. Then an old-timer in the doorway edged forward.

'Lookin' for the gal?' he enquired.

''Course I am, you old fool!' Brock blazed at him.

'I see'd her go, 'bout the time the cattle was stampedin' down the street. There was a guy with her, the one we tried to hang. Corbett, wasn't it?'

'They were together?' Brock demanded.

'Sure they were, on a horse.'

Brock gripped the old man's neck fiercely. 'Why the devil didn't you tell me they were escaping?'

'I couldn't git to you with all them cattle — Let go of my neck, Mr Brock. You're chokin' me.'

Brock flung the old man away from him savagely and then swung round.

'All right, Corbett's got away with Lucy,' he said. 'Right now he might be just any place and he's got a good start on us. Ted, get the cattle back where they belong and I'll follow you. The rest of you start right now and find Corbett and Lucy. *Get* him, even if you have to stay out for weeks!'

Promptly the assembly broke up — and at that moment Len Corbett was in the midst of completing the journey back to his hide-out, Saddles bringing up the rear. At the entrance to the cave, Len finally halted and helped the girl to alight. She looked at the cave opening with interest.

'So this is where you've been keeping yourself?'

Len turned from tethering his horse. 'Yes, thanks to Saddles. He's stood by me right from the beginning of this trouble.'

'Shucks,' Saddles grinned, dismounting. 'Bin a pleasure to make Brock uncomfortable.'

Len escorted the girl into the cave. She sat down thankfully on a chunk of rock and surveyed in the dim light.

'Home from home,' she commented. 'What's the idea of that boulder tied in the roof?'

'Just a precaution,' Len smiled; then he became serious again. 'Lucy, I snatched you from Brock because I couldn't stand the idea of your marrying him, but maybe it was a selfish viewpoint. Perhaps it's the one thing you ought to do if you're to get security.'

Saddles came into the cave, then glanced outside. 'Maybe I'd better keep watch,' he said, thinking.

'Definitely,' Lucy told him. 'Caleb will leave nothing unturned from now on.'

Saddles nodded and departed. Len moved across the cave, ill at ease.

'Care for something to eat?'

'No thanks. Not long since I had lunch.'

Abruptly Len took the girl's hand impulsively. 'Look, Lucy, I realize there's a few things that want explaining. I told you I was going to reform. It must look as though I've broken my promise.'

'I'm afraid it does. First you're going

to reform, then I hear about the cattle steal at the Maitland ranch.'

'I had no intention of taking part, even though I was present with the boys. There was no other way by which I could keep up with Brock.'

'Keep *up* with him?'

'I told you I was hunting for the man who'd burned down my spread and murdered my wife and son. That man is Brock.'

'I see . . . ' Lucy's voice was quiet. 'Well, as far as we are concerned it seems I jumped to the wrong conclusion. Somehow, I couldn't really believe you'd break your word like that. I believed enough in you to contrive your release from the necktie party.'

'You more than *believed* in me, Lucy, to take that risk!'

Lucy sat looking at him for a moment, then suddenly she got up from the rock. His arms closed around her as they kissed — not once, but many times.

'That was a lot of rubbish I talked

about taking on Caleb because of his money,' she said earnestly. 'I felt piqued by your behaviour and it was the only explanation I could think of. The part that worries me is that in exacting revenge you'll become a murderer, too. And two wrongs don't make a right.'

'I've no intention of murdering him, any more than I have hurt anybody else during my career as an outlaw. I want to nab him on a perfectly legal charge and have a marshal deal with him. That may take time, but sooner or later he'll walk into the trap. I'm convinced of it.'

'Not Caleb. He's too wily for that.'

'Wily or otherwise, all men love power — and finally overreach themselves. So will Brock one day. Might mean my own arrest if I'm recognized, but I'll chance that. I've got to bring Brock to trial. With the evidence which the authorities have already collected, and my own assertions about a seaman's knot — to say nothing of Brock's early connections with a fishing fleet — he'll be nailed all right. Then I guess I'll have done all I can to avenge my wife and son.'

'Yes,' Lucy acknowledged slowly. 'Yes, I guess you will. And what happens in the meantime?'

'We'll stay here for the moment. I'll fix you a shakedown and screen it off. You can share the chow we've got. When it begins to run out we'll have to think of something fresh.'

So it was decided. Saddles and Len agreed to take lookout in shifts, day and night, and Lucy would attend to the trivial domestic needs. The rest of the time she spent with Len ... Twice during the day, search parties came dangerously near the hide-out, and then went away again. They were on the job all night too, sometimes working with torches, but yet again they missed the vital spot. It was in the middle of the next morning when the trio, surveying from their high vantage point, watched a weary party of men and horses taking the trail slowly from Ransom's Bend.

'That may be the last of 'em for the

time being,' Saddles commented. 'They can't keep going over the same spot time and again. Finding us'll be too much like a needle in a haystack, I reckon.'

'To be hoped so,' Lucy answered, still in the torn wedding dress since she had nothing else to wear. 'I would be glad if I could get some more serviceable clothes from somewhere. Either of you two boys any suggestions?'

'Might try robbin' the general store,' Saddles mused. 'I'll have a stab at it tonight if you like. I'm too old a hand at the game to get caught.'

'I don't like it,' Lucy said, surprisingly. 'I've got a better idea. Suppose I went back into town myself?'

The two men stared at her in amazement.

'I mean it,' she insisted. 'What you want to know, Len, is when Caleb is going into action again, isn't it? How do you propose to find out about it?'

'Dunno. Have to think of something. What's that got to do with you going into town?'

'Everything. Suppose I spread the tale that I was snatched away from the wedding against my will? Suppose I go one further and say that you are dead? Shot in a gun-fight with Saddles, after which I limped back into town for the protection of Caleb. It can't miss, and knowing him as I do I'm pretty sure he'll believe it.'

'Then what?' Len asked, grim-faced. 'He'll have you married to him and we'll be back where we started.'

'Not quite. I can plead exhaustion and need of resting up. That will delay the marriage for the time being. While he's waiting I'm pretty sure that Caleb will organize a cattle-steal somewhere. If he does that I'll find out the details and let you know in advance.'

'By what means? One ride out of town and Brock will be on to you like a shot.'

'I'll take good care he doesn't know anything about it. I'll make such a convincing show of being glad to return that he won't bother to keep a watch on me.'

'And how will you find out if he's going to do a cattle-steal?' Saddles asked, thinking. 'He won't be likely to confide in you, will he?'

'No, but his boys will know all about it. I'll get it out of them — probably from Lefty. He was always a sucker for a woman.'

'Yes, perhaps so.' Len knitted his brows. 'I'm not saying that I like it, Lucy, because I have the feeling that something will go wrong some place.'

'It won't,' the girl assured him. 'I know what I'm doing. If you, Saddles, will give me a ride to within two miles of Ransom's Bend I'll walk the rest of the distance while you ride back to the mountains here. Make it tonight because there's less chance of us being seen, even though the search party does seem to have given up the struggle.'

'OK,' Saddles shrugged. 'If that's the way you want it.'

There was nothing either man could

do about it. Lucy's mind was made up, so the only thing to hope for was that she would not run into serious trouble anywhere. Len was not too sure about this. He brooded on it for the remainder of the day, but the girl did not change her mind and, at sundown, she was ready.

Saddles brought up his horse and Len lifted the girl into the saddle. She gave him an encouraging smile.

'It'll work,' she assured him. 'I know it will. Besides, I want to feel I've played my part in bringing a conviction.'

Len kissed her. 'All right, but I sure won't have an easy moment all the time you're away.'

She patted his hand and said no more. Saddles swung up behind her and nudged the horse forward. Len watched them go down the long declivity in the dying light and kept his eyes on them until they were out of sight in the mountain shadow and approaching night. Then he settled down to the task of watching for a possible search party.

In point of fact, a search party was on the move — and had been since sunset, taking an entirely new route. It was this new route which saved Saddles and the girl from running into them, but inevitably there came a time when the posse came across the trail Saddles and the girl had made.

'One way the trail leads to the mountains, and the other they veer off to the left,' Sheriff Hoyle mused, studying the trails in the torchlight. 'Looks like a well-loaded horse was making for Ransom's Bend, and taking a detour to do it.'

'Probably two on one horse,' Ted Realing commented.

The sheriff pondered for a moment, then came to a decision.

'Half us follow the trail to Ransom's Bend, and the other half to the mountains. Let's go!'

Immediately the party split up. Those left behind, which included the sheriff and Lefty, considered for a moment.

'Look,' Lefty said, 'what do we hope to git out this, Sheriff? The tracks distinctly showed that the rider — or riders — wus heading *away* from these mountains. We ain't going to find much even if we follow 'em through.'

'There's *three* people we're lookin' for,' the sheriff said. 'Corbett, Saddles, and Lucy Lee. No horse would carry more 'n two at a time. That leaves *one* somewheres, most probably in these mountains. Find that one, and we'll darned soon find the remainder. We'd better not *all* start pokin' around the mountains. Our quarry can see us quicker than we can see him and might give us the slip. You, Lefty, had better go alone. See what you can do. We'll stop here in case he makes a dash.'

Lefty nodded, and rode ahead. He reached the foothills and began to ascend, following the trail, unaware that Len Corbett was watching every move he made. Presently the rocks hid Lefty from view so Len took the only course:

he retired into the cave, his gun ready, to await developments.

Altogether it took Lefty half an hour to pursue the trail to its conclusion; then grinning to himself he rode back to where Sheriff Hoyle and the boys were waiting.

'I found it!' Lefty exulted. 'A horse, which looks like Corbett's, and a cave — in which Corbett may be hiding. I ain't taking the risk myself. Let's go and see.'

They all began moving; half way up the slope they dismounted, hobbled their horses, and continued on foot. When they reached the summit of the rise and had the rimrock before them Hoyle weighed up the situation.

'That cave?' he asked, noting the sleeping horse beside it.

'Yeah. I'll gamble Corbett's in there — mebbe asleep.'

Hoyle's hand tightened on his gun and he advanced very slowly. But quiet though he and the rest of the men were, they could not possibly avoid kicking one or two stones in their progress, and these faint sounds alerted Len to instant action.

'Corbett, if you're inside the cave, come out!' Hoyle shouted suddenly. 'Give yourself up. If you don't we'll come in and get you.'

Silence. Len inside the cave, gave a hard smile and waited.

'One more chance,' Hoyle called out, but the result was the same as before.

He jerked his head to the men and went forward cautiously, his gun at the ready. Behind him came Lefty, then the three other men who made up the party. Hoyle reached the cave mouth and stopped.

'Looks as though there ain't nobody here — ' he began, then he broke off with a yell of fear as something grey and shapeless came hurtling out of the cave depths straight at him.

He had not the chance to move. A rock, somehow tethered, struck him full in the chest and wiped him off the rimrock. Petrified with amazement his followers watched him hurtle into space and then turn head over heels as he crashed down into the depths of the chasm beyond. A dying scream pierced the quiet; Len's horse whinnied with the sudden disturbance — then all was quiet again. The mysterious flying boulder had vanished.

'Hell!' Lefty muttered, drawing a hand across his face. 'What in tarnation happened?'

He had not the kind of mind to think it out, so instead he plunged forward into the cave with his gun ready. Just in time he saw that boulder coming for him, and sidestepped. It missed him by a fraction and swung back. Then he tumbled to the trick. At the same moment Len's gun blazed savagely and chipped pieces out of the rocks.

'Take it easy!' Lefty snapped, firing blindly into the dark.

With his free hand he whipped out his knife and in the momentary pause slashed through the rope which held the boulder. It came crashing down at his feet just as the other men came in.

'One step more,' came Len's voice, 'and I'll blast the lot of you off that rimrock!'

Lefty listened intently to where the voice was coming from and then fired back. The bullet twanged on rock. Evidently Len had moved in the interval. He had. Used to the blackness of the cave he could see exactly where he was going, and at the present moment he was crouched far to one side, watching the group in the entrance.

'Right, open up!' Lefty ordered. 'We'll — '

He got no further. A powerful arm closed under his chin and a gun bedded hard in the small of his back.

'Drop your gun!' Len ordered. 'Go on, *drop* it!'

Unable to help himself Lefty did as he was told. His gun clattered down and the rest of the men hesitated, unable to fire with Lefty as a shield for their target.

'Down with your guns, the lot of you!' Len snapped. 'Make it quick.'

After a moment the men obeyed. Len proceeded to bundle the cursing Lefty outside. The others followed him, their hands raised.

'Now keep going!' Len ordered, bundling Lefty away from him. 'Get to your horses, and if you know what's good for you don't come back!'

The men continued their steady retreat, but not half so fast as Len would have liked. Abruptly he became aware of a sound behind him . . . it was nothing. Only his horse moving restlessly.

Slowly the men moved back — and still back, until at last they reached their horses. Disarmed, and beaten for the moment, they rode away into the night. With a grim face Len watched them go.

5

It was towards eleven o'clock when a tattered and dirty young woman slowly appeared in the main street of Ransom's Bend and made her stumbling way towards the Lazy Gelding. Partly she was putting on an act, and partly it was genuine. She was tired out with a pre-arranged three mile walk to the town, from where she had left Saddles, and again her high-heeled shoes were worse than useless in soft sand. The dirt and general untidiness were added specially for the occasion.

When she entered the saloon the patrons stared in genuine amazement. They were accustomed to seeing Lucy Lee as a cool, calm, well-dressed young woman. This tired and besmirched creature with her wedding dress in shreds was something new. Silently, eyes followed her as she limped towards the bar counter.

'What in heck — ?' The barkeep's eyes opened wide. 'It couldn't be Lucy come back?'

'It could, and it is. Give me a brandy and let Mr Brock settle for it.'

The brandy came up immediately. Lucy downed it, coughed a little, and then straightened up.

'Another?' Harry asked.

'No thanks. Where's Mr Brock?'

'Last I saw of him, he was in his office.'

Lucy nodded and shambled wearily across the pool room to the office, ignoring the stares which followed her. She did not knock on the door but went straight in and closed the door behind her. Brock, busy at his desk, glanced up and then stared fixedly.

'Lucy!'

'Right!' she assented, flopping in a chair. 'And I'm about all in, Caleb. Or maybe you've noticed?'

He got up and came around to her quickly. 'Well, what's the explanation?

Last I saw of you, you were vanishing through the church skylight. Later I heard that you'd ridden off with Len Corbett.'

Lucy thought swiftly. 'I didn't ride off with him. He kidnapped me.'

'Then what?'

'He took me to his hide-out in the mountains. Saddles was there as well.'

'That was the night before last,' Brock said deliberately. 'You were there quite a long time.'

'No longer than I could help. I had to watch my chance to make a getaway, and finally it came. I managed to dodge Saddles when he rode off somewhere to look for water, and as for Len . . . well, I shot him. There was no other way to get free. He happened to turn his hip towards me and I snatched his gun.'

'He was stripped of his guns at the hanging,' Brock said.

'I know. Saddles gave me one of his.'

Brock did not comment. He dragged up a chair with his foot and lighted a cheroot, looking at the girl with his little eyes.

'Then I'm to assume that Corbett is dead?' he asked finally.

'That's the way I left him. I bolted for it, and I've had to tramp all the way across the desert back to town.'

'Don't mind me saying it, but I'm surprised you came back.'

'Where else could I go?' Lucy asked, spreading her hands. 'I had no alternative.'

That was true enough. Brock considered for a while, and guessing what was passing through his mind Lucy took the initiative.

'I've told you the truth, Caleb — believe me!' She slipped to his knees and grasped his hand. 'I sort of didn't realize how well off I was before.'

'How do you mean?'

'The way I've treated you. I've not done the right thing, and now I'm sure of it. I admit that I had a sort of crush on Len, and that was one reason why I released him from the hanging — but

I've seen since how wrong I was. I'm glad — really glad — to come back.'

For the first time Brock's ugly face broke into a smile. He raised the girl slowly.

'OK, that's good enough for me. Perhaps in some ways it's done good you made the break. For one thing it's shown you the error of your ways, and for another it's bin the means of disposing of Corbett. I guess I can call off the boys from the search party.'

Lucy hesitated. 'But you *have*, haven't you? I saw them all trailing back long ago, completely beaten.'

'When exactly?'

'About the middle of this morning.'

'Oh, that! Yeah, after the all-night search. Matter of fact I packed 'em off again after a short rest. This evening. It's a wonder you didn't see 'em.'

'No. I — I took a long detour. I didn't follow the main trail.'

Brock was silent for a long moment, then he said, 'Well, we can get married as we originally intended, and nobody likely to disturb us this time. The minister is staying in Ransom's Bend for the moment. I kept him here just in case I happened to find you.'

Lucy nodded slowly, holding the back of the chair for support. She was still putting on her act.

'Where are you staying since your ranch was burned down?' she asked.

'Cactus Hotel, down the main street. Anyway, that's beside the point. Tomorrow, or the day after at the latest, we'll get married.'

'And take me to the Cactus Hotel to live? I'm not sure I like the idea of that.'

'Mmm, I hadn't thought of that,' Brock admitted.

'Leave the marriage for a while,' Lucy went on. 'I'm too tired to think about it at present anyway. Guess I'll go and get some sleep.'

'Yeah — you do that.' Brock kissed her fiercely and she accepted it without flinching; then he watched her trail slowly from the office and shut the door.

Slowly he sat down to think things out. It was about ten minutes later when Lefty came in, following a brief knock on the door.

'Well?' Brock asked, looking up. 'You've not got Saddles, I suppose?'

'Saddles?' Lefty looked wondering. 'I ain't even seen him. We split in half to follow a trail and then joined up again near town. We got a trail that led from Ransom's Bend — about three miles outside it — to the foothills. But why should you be concerned about Saddles?'

It was Brock's turn to look surprised. 'Because Saddles is the only one left. With Corbett dead you've naturally — '

'Corbett *dead*?' Lefty repeated. 'When did this happen?'

'Early this evening some time — '

'For your information, Mr Brock, the only reason we've come back is to git reinforcements. Corbett's very much alive. We found his hide-out and he completely got the drop on us. He threw the sheriff into a canyon with some kind of rock gadget . . . '

'Say that again,' Brock requested slowly, so Lefty did so with a little more detail. When he had finished Brock was pale with fury.

'And you didn't see Saddles any place?'

'Nope. May have bin his trail which we followed.'

'It *was* his trail no shadow of doubt about it, and the extra heavy imprints were caused by the horse carrying Lucy Lee as well. She told me she had shot Corbett.'

'Huh? Lucy did? You mean she's come back?'

'Yes. And I can see now just how. Saddles must have brought her almost to the town, and she walked the rest. She said she'd shot Corbett. That he's dead.'

'Then she's a liar,' Lefty said bluntly.

'I wonder what her game is,' Brock mused. 'I'd better find out — and quick.'

'Yeah. You sure must. But look, boss,

about more men . . . do I get 'em? Since the sheriff was killed I've sort of taken charge.'

Surprisingly, Brock shook his head. 'No; leave him be for the moment. Like as not he'll have shifted his headquarters now he knows we're on to him. I'll see you later about it. I've other things to do.'

'OK,' Lefty shrugged; then, looking rather puzzled he left the office.

Brock followed immediately behind him, delegated Harry, the barkeep, to do the locking up, then went on his way to the little house at the end of the street where Lucy had a room. Mrs Cranby opened the door to him.

'Well, Mr Brock!' She seemed surprised. 'Anything wrong?'

'Plenty. Lucy's come home, I believe?'

'Why sure. She went straight to bed — '

Brock strode into the small hallway. 'I've got to see her. Which is her room?'

'First on the left upstairs. But do you think you . . . '

Brock was not even listening. He

strode up the stairs, reached the girl's room, and thumped loudly on the door.

'Yes?' came Lucy's voice. 'Who is it?'

'Caleb. I want a word with you.'

'Then come in. The door isn't locked.'

Brock obeyed and closed the door sharply behind him. He was checked for a moment by the gloom; then he found the oil lamp and lighted it. Lucy, sitting up in bed, looked at him in surprise.

'Well, there's nothing like being informal,' she said drily.

Brock turned slowly, his face grim. There was a look in his small grey eyes which made Lucy's heart beat more swiftly.

'What were you handing me when you said you shot Corbett?' he demanded.

The girl was silent, staring at him.

'You'd better answer me,' he said softly. 'If you don't, I'll give you hell.'

He crossed to the door, turned the key swiftly, and then put it in his pocket. He returned to the bedside.

'What game have you got on?' he insisted. 'Like as not you didn't tramp from the mountains. You came with Saddles and he dropped you off — close to town. Then you put on an act.'

Lucy was silent, her hands working on the coverlet.

'Answer me!' Brock roared. 'Don't sit like a deaf-mute.'

Lucy fingered her lip for a moment, then looked up sullenly.

'All right, so I did ride with Saddles to within a few miles of the town — and I didn't shoot Len Corbett. I gave him the slip. Saddles was willing to help me get away from Corbett. I came back for one thing only, to get security. I didn't think you'd ever believe me if I told the truth, so I invented the bit about shooting Corbett.'

'Which wasn't very smart,' Brock sneered. 'I still think there's a good deal more to it than what you've told me, but maybe I'll find out in time what it is. In the meanwhile we'll step up those marriage arrangements. You're being married tomorrow afternoon. Savvy?'

'But I'm too exhausted — '

'Oh no you're not!' Brock snapped. 'Come to my office tomorrow morning and collect the necessary for a new wedding dress.'

He turned to the door and unlocked it, then paused as a thought struck him.

'There'll be somebody watching your moves from now on, so don't try any funny business.'

With that he went and closed the door sharply. Lucy remained exactly where she was, staring bitterly into space.

★ ★ ★

Also about this time Len was intently watching a lone rider coming in towards the foothills. He only relaxed when he realized it was Saddles. Some minutes later Saddles' horse came panting to the top of the slope and picked its way along the rimrock.

'Well, what gives?' Len asked, as

Saddles dismounted.

'Quite a few things, I guess.' Saddles adjusted the feeding bag on the horse's nose and then turned. 'I nearly got meself captured.'

'Oh? What happened?'

'Just as I was riding away from Ransom's Bend after dropping Lucy I saw a crowd of the boys ahead of me. Fortunately they were coming slowly and keepin' their eyes on the ground — followin' my trail marks. I rode away pronto to the nearest rocky stretch I could find and made the trail vanish at that point — then I rode hell for leather back here. I don't suppose they'll trace anythin' this far.'

'The other half did,' Len said grimly.

'Huh? What other half?'

'The other half of the search party. Lefty was amongst them. I've been having fun and games, even to the extent of knocking Sheriff Hoyle into the chasm there.'

Saddles said nothing as he led the way into the cave, then he asked, 'You got out of the mess all right?'

'Sure. I'm still here. I sent the gang packing and because there weren't enough to cause trouble they rode back to town. But they'll be back, dozens strong, and we shan't be able to hold 'em. That being so we'll change our hide-out and go to the further end of the foothills. When Lucy comes to tell us something we'll see her first and go and get her. Incidentally, how did Lucy make out? Drop her OK?'

'Sure. Quite near to town. I guess the rest is up to her. She doesn't seem the kind of girl who'll flunk anything.'

Len was silent for a moment or two, then he moved restlessly.

'We'd better explore for fresh quarters. Come on.'

Leaving their horses where they were they started an exploration on foot. They went for perhaps two miles, following treacherous rimrocks, when they found the mountain sides closing in all around them. Finally they came to a halt within an extremely narrow area, high above a valley, with a cave mouth looming a dozen yards away from them. To reach it demanded traversing a narrow ledge.

'We can only just see the desert from that cave,' Len commented, coming to a stop. 'It's a swell hide-out, anyways. Somehow, the place looks familiar, yet I can't quite place it.'

'I can. It's Vulture's Pass, viewed from above. Last time we saw it we were down below.'

'Why, of course!' suddenly Len remembered how, on the night when they had attempted the rustling of Maitland's Ranch, they had detoured to examine this very pass, through which they had been expected to drive cattle later on.

'Yep,' Saddles confirmed, staring up at the heights, 'it's it all right.'

They surveyed again, noting the extreme narrowness of the valley below. As Len had estimated at the time, it would not be possible to drive more than three cattle abreast, so confined were the walls.

'See what the cave's like,' Len said, advancing again.

It proved to be pretty similar to the one they had left, and there was just enough room for the horses outside. If it came to it, they would have a far better chance to defend themselves in the narrow space than in the former retreat.

'OK, it'll do,' Saddles decided, when the survey was complete. 'Have to use a shoehorn to git us out of here — even granting they trace us this far. Get a fair view of the desert too. And there's something else . . . '

'What?'

'If Brock ever does decide to rustle some cattle again they'll have to come through here if he wants to get them to Medicine Point. He made that clear to us. We might figure something out to trap them in this bottle-neck and — who knows? — mebbe Brock as well. He'll have a helluva job tryin' to talk himself out of that.'

'Yeah,' Len agreed thoughtfully. 'Mebbe

you've got something there — '

He stopped abruptly. He had been looking towards the desert. For a second or two he thought he saw something moving in the mist; and in another moment he was sure. A lone horseman travelling at high speed towards the foothills, and obviously not sure of his direction since he came to a halt now and again and looked about him.

'Now who the heck's *that*?' Saddles questioned. 'A one-man posse is a new one on me — and it ain't Lucy. Mighty strange.'

They stood watching as the lone rider came closer to the foothills, still obviously unsure of himself. Then, faintly on the night air, came a cry.

'Corbett! Cor — bett! I've news for you.'

'This a trick?' Len muttered suspiciously.

Saddles did not answer. He drew his gun just in case.

'No, take it easy.' Len put a hand on his arm. 'No use giving away our position — and besides we only shoot in self-defence.'

'For cryin' out loud!' Saddles ejaculated, as the dim figure of the rider waved something in the starlight which looked like a white duster. It was a duster, or a towel. It became quite distinct as it unfurled.

'Corbett, if you're around, say something!' came a shout.

'That guy means it,' Len decided abruptly. 'That's a flag of truce, but I don't know whether he'll honour it: Go back along the rim and then we'll give him a shout. We'll keep him covered as he comes up.'

They moved quickly back along the ledge so as to give no clue as to their intended hide-out. When eventually they came to a clear spot in the foothills Len gave a shout.

'Hello there! Who are you?'

The rider wheeled his horse. The fluttering whiteness of his 'banner' was now clearly visible.

'Corbett, I've news for you. I'm Harry,

the barkeep at the Lazy Gelding.'

'What *is* this?' Saddles muttered, scratching his neck.

'Do no harm to find out.' Len raised his voice in a shout. 'OK, Harry, follow my voice, I'll respect your flag of truce as long as you do. One slip and you're finished. Come on.'

Harry obeyed immediately. Just here the upward climb was not too difficult. Finally he came up, guided by Len's voice, still with his flag of truce fluttering in the wind. Len and Saddles kept their guns ready and waited.

'Well?' Len asked curtly. 'What do you want?'

'There's nothing I want, but there's some news which I think you should have. Because you've got to have it quick I rode out specially from Ransom's Bend when the saloon had shut down, on the chance that I might find you. This is my polishing cloth,' he added, looking at his flag of truce.

'OK, start talkin'.' Len put his gun away. 'I reckon you and me never quarrelled, Harry, so let's have it.'

'It's about Lucy Lee. Brock's discovered most of her trickery, and he came back to the saloon tonight sayin' he's going to marry her tomorrow afternoon. He tipped me off to get the drinks ready for the celebration.'

Len's face became grim. 'Tomorrow afternoon, eh? Come to think of it, why do you put yourself out to come and tell me this? What's the catch?'

'No catch, Corbett — honest. I'm doing it because I like Miss Lee and I think she's bin having too many bad breaks. The way Brock treats her is nobody's business. He thrashed her recently in case you don't know — and I dare say he gave her hell tonight from what he was sayin'. Besides, I don't like Brock, and never did. He's a no-account skunk.'

'Yuh can say that again,' Saddles murmured.

'I dunno what you'll do about Lucy,' Harry shrugged, 'but at least I've told you what's cookin'. Now I'd best be getting back. Nobody's likely to have missed me since the saloon's closed at this time.'

'Right,' Len said gratefully. 'And thanks for the tip off. I'll think of something. Brock will never have Lucy for his wife even if I have to burn down the whole darned town and minister too.'

'OK,' Harry grinned. 'And best of luck.'

He swung the horse's head, refolded the polishing cloth, and rode back down the slope. Len stood musing and watched him go.

'Kinda complicates things,' Saddles said at length.

'Yeah. I've got to think of something — and quick. In the meantime, here's another idea. Fix this valley so both ends can be sealed at a moment's notice.'

'Huh?'

'Sooner or later,' Len said deliberately, 'Brock is going to drive cattle through here. We don't know that he'll accompany the rustling gang, but it's a possibility that he will because he's nobody he can really trust to do the job properly. He was going to leave that to me: now he's only got Lefty and I don't think Lefty has the brains to do the thing on his own.'

'So?'

'If we can trap the cattle, and those responsible for stealing 'em in this valley, we've got something. We need a marshal from Medicine Point to see the whole thing for himself. If we don't get Brock we'll force the boys — or the marshal will — to tell who put them up to it. If we *do* get Brock, all the better. The marshal may have to wait some time, but that's his job. Just as long as he gets his man.'

'Mmm,' Saddles murmured uneasily. 'That part's all right, but what about *us*?'

'Us? How do you mean?'

'Don't forget we're wanted men as well. As soon as a marshal sees either you or me in Medicine Point there's going to be trouble. We'll end up in jail!'

'Don't you believe it. There have been reward notices out for a band of outlaws — us — but nobody's ever seen our faces. We've always been masked. There's no proof, and even if there were and one of us got jailed, the marshal would still look into the matter of Brock because it's his duty. No, I don't reckon there's much to worry over on that score. We're going to take the chance — or at least you are. You're going to fetch the marshal.'

'OK,' Saddles agreed, though he did not look too happy.

'It's our only chance to nab Brock,' Len insisted. 'Apart from the cattle-thieving, which has already been reported to the authorities at Medicine Point, there's the bigger charge of burning down my ranch and murdering my wife and son.'

Saddles nodded, but he did not say anything.

'Undoubtedly cattle will come through that valley when Brock does any more stealing,' Len went on, musing. 'It's a short cut, and the easiest way. Our job is to find a method of cutting off both ends so neither man nor beast can get out before a marshal is onto them. We'd better see the topmost heights and judge what can be done.'

Turning, he began the climb to the upper levels of the mountains, and Saddles clambered after him. Finally they were at the highest point of the ramparts marking the Ransom's Bend side of the valley. Down below, the valley itself was a void, with the mountain peaks opposite.

'Ain't much we can do, far as I can see,' Saddles commented. 'The only chance would be to start an avalanche, and that would take dynamite. It'd blow the entire face of this mountain into the valley and there wouldn't be anybody could escape over the rubble. Mebbe it'd even bury them.'

'Probably so,' Len admitted. 'And the other end of the valley is about the same for width. Dynamite at each end and fired simultaneously would form an effective blockage. That would seem to be the answer.'

'But we ain't *got* any dynamite!'

'I know that, but there's an ammo dump adjoining the livery stable back in Ransom's Bend. Plenty of dynamite sticks there. Brock himself told us about it on the night of the Maitland raid, but mebbe you've forgotten. I haven't. We're going to grab off some of that dynamite.'

'Yeah? When?'

'Tonight. You're going to ride back here with it and fix it in position. I'll stay in and around Ransom's Bend ready to do something about Lucy. I don't know what right now, but *something*. Now we'd better be goin'.'

★   ★   ★

It was well into the night when Len and Saddles reached the main street of Ransom's Bend. They drew rein and looked about them.

'Like a tomb,' Len commented. 'Just

173

the way we want it.'

'Want me to stay here, or come with you?' Saddles asked.

'Better come with me.'

They moved silently into the night. Entry into the ammo dump did not prove much of a problem. They selected the sticks they wanted, returned with them to their horses, and loaded up the saddle-bags. Then they left the ammo dump door as they had found it.

'OK,' Len breathed, with a sigh of relief. 'Now you get going. When you've set the dynamite, ride out and fetch a marshal. Take my saddle-bag with you.'

'And what do you aim to do?'

'I'm going to think things out — concerning Lucy, I mean. Leave me be.'

Saddles said no more. Gingerly he transferred Len's saddle-bag to his own horse, then — still exercising extreme caution — he set off. With a grim smile Len watched him out of sight in the starlight, then he came back to the problem in hand.

How to save Lucy from the approaching marriage? A second stampede would never work. In that case, why not the *obvious* thing? A hold-up! From an outlaw that was about what one would expect. Len grinned to himself as the idea came to him. He could spend the night here — in fact he could stay quite a time with the provisions he'd brought with him. Then on the morrow he would act.

He nodded to himself and set about the job of finding somewhere safe to spend the night. He found a settling place a little distance out of town, and the night passed undisturbed.

He breakfasted quickly before there was a likelihood of anybody coming his way, and then got on the move. Finally he selected an outcropping of trees as his sanctuary for the day. Noon came. He scraped together some of his provisions, took some water, and then prepared for action. Drawing his kerchief up over his face he rode deliberately towards the town, stopping half a mile from it and hobbling his horse. The remainder of the journey he made on foot, his eyes alert for the least sign of danger. None showed itself. So eventually he reached the main street and, his gun in his hand, stood surveying from the concealment of a building.

There were plenty of people about, most of them drifting towards the other end of the town. Since the church was situated there it seemed logical to Len that they were potential spectators. From his point of view he could not see the church so he moved on again, dodging behind the backs of buildings, ready to use his gun if he were approached.

Luck held. He succeeded in getting to the further end of the town, and at the rear of the church paused to consider. There was nobody just here, but from the sounds which floated to him there was evidently plenty going on in front. Quickly he surveyed the roof. No use going up there. After the last occasion it would probably be well guarded.

Eventually he came to a rear door, drawn to but not locked. Very cautiously he opened it and waited for a moment or two. Nothing happened. A buzz of conversation floated to him, evidently from within the church. Finally, he peered cautiously through the crack. He was at the pulpit end of the church. He could just see it, and a stretch of the front row of people beyond. Then something else moved into his line of vision — the back view of the minister from Medicine Point, attired in the official garb of the clergy. He was gravely contemplating a Bible.

A church was definitely no place to start trouble, but it had to be done. Silently Len slipped inside and crouched down at the rear of the somewhat decrepit harmonium. It was not playing at the moment, but a tight-jacketed individual was all prepared for action — and suddenly it came, blasting Len's ears with the noise.

He examined his gun quickly and

then peered round the end of the harmonium. His lips tightened. Brock, once again in his wedding regalia, was already in position — and Lucy was coming down the aisle with a small party grouped about her. Nobody seemed to be armed, as indeed they hardly would be at such a function, which was the one thing Len hoped for.

He waited until Lucy had almost completed her journey down the aisle, then he suddenly put himself in full view, standing a little behind the minister. Brock saw him immediately, and his amazement was complete: then just as quickly it turned to fury.

'How the hell — ' he began, and the minister raised his head in shocked surprise.

'Mr Brock, in a house of God such language is — '

'Hold it, Parson,' Len said curtly, stepping forward and digging the gun in the minister's back. 'I've got a little talkin' to do myself around here. I'll put it plainly: Caleb Brock ain't going to marry Lucy Lee.'

'Who says so?' Brock roared; then he swung round to his minions on the front row. 'What are you mugs doing just sittin' looking? Here's Corbett for the asking. Go and get him!'

None of the men moved, although they stood up. Lefty was amongst them, feeling inside his makeshift suit for a gun.

'Draw that gun, Lefty, and you're a dead man,' Len warned. 'This may be a house of God, but I'll shoot just the same. I'm takin' this risk for only one reason — to protect a girl who's a darned sight too good for any of you, 'specially you, Caleb Brock!'

Brock could do nothing but stand and tremble with rage. Gazing into that cold blue gun muzzle was unnerving.

'Lucy, come here,' Len said at length. 'Get right behind me.'

She did not even hesitate, but as she came past, Brock made a lightning grab at her and swung her in front of him.

'Now — shoot if you dare!' he challenged.

Len hesitated and glanced sharply about him. That second lost him his opportunity. With a lightning blow of his arm the minister knocked the gun out of Len's hand, and instantly Lefty and the boys leapt forward. Len did not stand a chance. He was seized and firmly held.

'Nice work,' Brock commented, relaxing and pushing Lucy away from him. 'There looks like being another interruption to our wedding, Parson, but business comes first. I'm going to settle this once and for all. I haven't the time to go through the formalities of a second hanging. I think it would be better if Len Corbett is left to think things over before he dies. Be a change from a quick escape.'

'What are you meaning to do?' Lucy asked slowly, and Brock grinned.

'Simple. Leave him to the desert. Don't know why I didn't think of it sooner. It's a far harder master than the rope — but there's one thing about it:

You can't fix the desert like you can a rope.'

'Are you sure that's a good idea, Mr Brock?' Lefty asked doubtfully. 'We want to be sure Corbett pays a hundred per cent.'

'He will,' Brock answered grimly. 'Bound and gagged, right out in the desert, no horse or water and only the sun for company. I reckon that's sure punishment.'

There was silence for a moment, the company looking at one another. Since Brock was boss of the town he'd undoubtedly have his way — and he did. Abruptly he turned to the two deputy sheriffs.

'You two take Corbett. Get your horses and ride him to as deserted a spot as you can find. Then dump him and come back. I reckon the sun will do the rest.'

Lucy made a half move, but Brock's iron grip held her back. Len himself merely smiled crookedly and then submitted to being bundled out of the

181

church by the deputies. Slowly Brock relaxed.

'Right,' he snapped, looking at the minister. 'There's been far too much delay. You ready?'

The cleric nodded uncomfortably. In the entire course of his ministry he had never encountered such interruption to a wedding.

'Well, go on!' Brock roared. 'Get busy!'

6

Saddles, quite unaware as yet of how badly things had gone awry, was about at the end of his job of dynamiting Vulture's Pass. It had been a long job, and a dangerous one, and it was well after noon when he finished. Now he surveyed the results of his handiwork. Not that there was much to see — only a projecting fuse from the rocks, roughly covered over the top to prevent any dew wetting it. At the other end of the pass there was the same setup. Once the two fuses were touched off the very face of the pass would lift outwards.

'Yeah,' Saddles murmured, wiping his face. 'I guess that's about the size of it. Time Len was showing up with Lucy, if he's done the thing proper.'

He surveyed the desert, beheld nothing of interest, so turned to the job of fixing a meal. He had already transferred everything from the previous hide-out to the new one, so it was not a job which took him long. Feeling quite satisfied with himself he settled down to canned meat while he waited for the coffee to warm up.

The desert lay stretched out before him, a shimmering haze of heat with the distant details obscured. Not a thing stirred. The outcroppings of cactus were motionless; overhead the sky was cloudless cobalt. It had reached the hour when the sun was about at its fiercest. Here in the shadow of the mountains Saddles was comfortable, shielded from the direct glare.

Then suddenly, in the act of raising a sandwich to his mouth, Saddles paused — not quite sure of what he saw. In a few moments it became clearer — three specks riding hard in the sunlight.

'So they're at it again, huh?' Saddles forgot all about his food and watched intently, fully expecting the trio would ride straight for the mountains. Then Saddles frowned. They were not coming towards the mountains at all, but heading away into the desert.

'I'd sure give something for a pair of field-glasses,' Saddles muttered. 'Wonder who those three saddle-tramps are?'

It was not possible at his distance to discern any details. He could only just make out that the objects were horsemen and that the three of them should be heading right into the desert, an acknowledged death trap, did not make sense. So they slowly faded into the haze and were gone.

'Must be strangers,' Saddles told himself, scratching his head, 'otherwise they'd sure know what they're getting into.'

He shrugged and continued with his interrupted lunch. He finished it, drank the coffee, and relaxed to consider the situation he was in. It was now a matter of waiting for Len and Lucy, and if that didn't mature he had the unenviable job of riding out to Medicine Point for a marshal.

He rolled out a cigarette, lighted it, and then sat musing. Then presently he gave a start. The three horsemen were reappearing out of the haze. No — not *three* horsemen: there were only two of them, leading a riderless horse between them, and they were moving fast.

'This doesn't make sense,' Saddles declared. 'There ain't no town the way those saddle-tramps took, so they couldn't ha' left the third man there. What the heck have they done with him?'

He got to his feet. In a matter of minutes the horsemen began to fade with distance and heat-haze as they rode hard in the direction of Ransom's Bend.

'Mighty queer,' Saddles reflected. 'In fact I'd say there's something here which isn't quite right. I reckon it can do no harm to look.'

Half an hour later he had picked up the trail of the horsemen in the soft sand of the true desert. It both came and went, stretching away into distance as a defilement in the natural smooth-ness of the sand. Puzzling to himself

Saddles jog-trotted his horse along steadily in the afternoon glare, until his head and eyes ached with the reflection of brilliance from the sand.

In fifteen minutes, where the trails ended, Saddles found himself looking at a black object. Finally, he was looking down at a solitary man, tightly bound hand and foot, and a gag fixed between his teeth. He had no hat and was sodden with sweat from the blazing glare overhead.

'Well, looky here!' Saddles slipped from his horse and stared blankly. 'Len!'

He wasted no further time. In a few moments he had the gag and ropes off, then he handed over the water bottle. Len sucked at it greedily and then panted for breath.

'A miracle,' he whispered. 'Nothing else but . . . ' He struggled to his feet.

'Miracle nothin'! I saw the whole thing. When three men trail out into the unexplored desert and only two of 'em come back with a riderless horse between 'em it makes you think. What *is* this? Some new idea of Brock's?'

'Yeah.' Len quickly fashioned his bandanna into a head covering. 'Brock had the idea of bringin' me out here to finish things off. Guess it would have worked too, if you hadn't turned up. Said he hadn't got time to stage a hanging — '

'An' has he married Lucy after all?'

'I'm afraid so. That's one point I've lost — an' it's a big point. Better give me a ride back while I think things over.'

'Sure thing.'

Len climbed to the saddle with Saddles behind him. As they rode back he made a comment.

'Good job you disobeyed orders.'

'Meaning what?' Saddles growled.

'Meaning that if you'd gone for a marshal like I told you I'd have been frying by now.'

Saddles said nothing, but he grinned widely. Then, when they reached the foothills, both he and Len dismounted and finished their journey on foot. While Saddles thereafter wiped down and watered the horse, Len had a meal and meditated meanwhile.

'What about the dynamite?' he asked. 'How did you make out?'

'Everything's set — both ends.'

'That's one good thing. As to the remainder, I just don't know how to act. I shan't go to Ransom's Bend again. Besides, it's better for Brock to think I'm dead. Seems nothing for it but to sit and wait for something to happen. If any cattle snatches are attempted, and the cattle come through this pass, we shall know without being told.'

'Yeah, but it may be weeks, or even months. If at all.'

'I don't see that there's anything we can do to hurry the issue. The only hope is that, thinking me dead and therefore unable to upset things, Brock will go to work fairly quickly. You'll have to go and get that marshal, Saddles. Anything may happen at any moment now the marriage business is finished with.'

'And what are you going to do? Stop here?'

'Nothing else I can do. While you're in Medicine Point you'd better get plenty of provisions. How much money have you got?'

'Enough for that, anyways. An' if I see Brock in my travels I'll shoot the tar outa him.'

'No — anything but that.' Len shook his head seriously. 'Can't I drum it into your skull that I want him *legally* accused of the murder of my wife and son? Killing him will only lay you open to a charge of murder and make things worse than ever.'

Saddles shrugged. 'Well, I'd better be on my way. Medicine Point is no small hop. Don't expect me back before some time tomorrow, and in the meantime, best of luck.'

Len nodded absently and Saddles swung to his horse. Then a thought seemed to strike him.

'Say, what about a horse? If you need one in a hurry how are you going to manage?'

'I dunno. Just have to put up with it. I'm not likely to move from here, anyhow.'

'I'd bring you one from Medicine Point, but horseflesh costs plenty of money.'

'Forget it. When you come back we can always ride double saddle in case of emergency.'

Saddles nodded and mounted. Then with a final wave he went on his way, slowly disappearing from Len's sight down the long, precipitous slope which led to the valley floor.

Way back in Ransom's Bend things were not quite so lonely or so peaceful. The wedding of Brock and Lucy had duly taken place and been followed by the celebrations which Brock had planned beforehand, commencing with a 'slap up' dinner at the local hotel, in which there seemed to be crowded every inhabitant of Ransom's Bend.

Not without reason, since Brock was paying for everything.

The one who should have been radiantly happy was distinctly the reverse. Lucy sat beside Brock, her eyes fixed on the wedding band on her finger. She ignored the raucous toasts, the compliments, and even the dinner — which, considering everything, was a surprisingly good one.

'What the devil's the matter with you?' Brock demanded, in an undertone. 'Take the damned miserable look off your face!'

'I would if I had reason to,' Lucy retorted. 'And I'll look how I like! You'll have to put up with it.'

Brock's lips tightened in fury. He deliberately kicked sideways under the table and the toe of his boot struck Lucy across the shin. She winced and shut her eyes but said nothing.

'Keep your chin up, kid,' murmured Harry, the barkeep, taking away Lucy's uneaten lunch. 'I'll stand by you if there's trouble.'

'Th-thanks, Harry.' He noticed that there were tears in her eyes as she glanced at him.

'What the hell do you *mean*? Stand by?' Brock rose unsteadily to his feet, his voice thick and his eyes inflamed. 'Do you think I didn't *hear* that, Harry?'

'I don't care if you did hear it,' Harry answered, with a frank stare. 'Seems to me Miss Lucy's in need of some protection around here.'

Brock's face twitched, but he was too drunk to find words to continue the argument. He sat down again heavily.

'Jus' goes to show,' he muttered. 'You have a man workin' for you for years, and then he gives you no co-operation. But I'll make yuh sit up for that remark, Harry. You'll smart for it later. You see if you don't!'

Harry took no notice. He was clearing crockery, with several of the hotel staff to help him; then there was a sudden disturbance from outside. The loud whinnying of a horse and something that sounded like a scuffle.

'What's going on?' Brock demanded, closing one eye to get things in focus. 'What's going *on*?'

Harry moved to the big window. What he saw outside made him grin privately to himself, but he had a straight face as he turned back into the room again.

Brock swayed to his feet, belched, then made his way unsteadily forward. He looked out of the window, blinked, and looked again. Then he gave a yell of anger, so loud it stopped the general conversation.

'Len Corbett's horse has escaped! Harry, why the hell didn't you say so?'

For a second there was silence, then one or two cowpokes — the deputies amongst them — hurried forward and looked outside. It was a fact that the horse, brought back after Len had been deposited in the desert, had pulled itself free of the tie rack and disappeared. Such was the instinct of the animal it evidently realized that it was a permanent separation from its master unless it did something. It *had* done something. It had gone completely.

'Better follow it,' one of the deputies said. 'Horseflesh is valuable. 'Sides, there's no telling what an intelligent animal like that might do. Might even set Corbett free.'

'Don't talk like fools!' Brock stormed. 'You can never catch a riderless horse, no matter how hard you try. It'll perhaps go to Corbett, but I doubt it. Leave it be. Mebbe I'll investigate myself later on. Right now I've more interesting things to do.'

He swung round, lurched, and moved across to where Lucy was sitting.

'Such as havin' a few moments with m' little bride,' he continued, seizing Lucy tightly by the shoulders and forcing her to kiss him. 'I reckon we — '

'Take your hands off her, Brock!'

Brock rose very slowly, helped by Lucy's pushing hands. She turned her face away while Brock focused on the one who had intervened. It was Harry, very quiet but determined.

'*What* did you say?' Brock gulped, a vein swelling in his neck.

'I told you to take your hands off her! You're that blind drunk you don't know what you're doing. Boss or no boss, no man's going to make himself offensive to a woman in my sight. I suggest you go home to Ma Cranby's.'

Lucy half got up, then Brock's iron hand clamped on her shoulder and forced her down again.

'Move frum that seat, Lucy, and you'll be sorry,' Brock warned. 'As for you, Harry, you've bin gettin' in my hair a mite too long. Mebbe it's time I did something about it.'

Nobody spoke. Every eye was fixed on the gathering storm. Then suddenly Brock flew into action, intoxicated though he was. He snatched at a nearby bottle and in one clean sweep brought it down on Harry's head with smashing force. The barkeep did not stand a chance. He collapsed, glass splinters around him, and blood oozing from his skull. Horrified, Lucy was the first one to reach him, regardless of Brock's threats. She raised Harry's head and shoulders as well as she could and gazed fixedly at the blood on her palm.

'You've — you've *killed* him!' she cried at last, grief and hatred nearly choking her. 'You're a murderer, Caleb, and everyone here's a witness — '

Before Lucy could finish she found herself elbowed out of the way as the deputy sheriff investigated. He looked up with a taut face.

'She's right, boss. He's dead.' He paused a moment and then looked at the men around him. 'Carry him to his home. We can't leave him here.'

Brock, sobered, drew a hairy paw down his face. 'I — didn't mean that to happen,' he whispered. 'Must ha' bin the way that I caught him.' His small grey eyes narrowed suddenly. 'But remember this, the lot of you! It was self defence. I'm boss of this town and nobody's goin' to pin a murder on me.'

Nobody spoke. The situation was

difficult — a case of the king could do no wrong. As Lord High Everything of Ransom's Bend, Brock was almost unassailable — even for murder.

'OK,' said one of the deputies, at length. 'It was an accident. We're agreed on that.'

The other men nodded slowly. They realized that if Brock were made to pay the price they would automatically be out of jobs. Money ranked far higher than justice.

'You — skunks,' Lucy breathed, staring round on the group. 'You ornery, yellow-livered skunks! Words like that don't come to me easy as a rule, but right now I'm meaning everything I say. You see a man murdered in front of your very eyes, and you're too scared to do anything about it. Harry was the only one with enough decency to try and stand for law and order in this filthy town. Yellow! The lot of you!'

With that she swung and headed for the door. She expected Brock to hurry over and stop her, but he didn't. He was standing motionless, trying to reason things out, more than a little shocked by the thing he had done. He had lost the confidence of the people, that much he knew. From now on he would have to hold them by brute force, or the game would be up.

'I reckon,' he said at length, pondering, 'that that brings the wedding celebration to an end. Bin a darned awkward sort of day with an unexpectedly tragic finish. First Len Corbett, and then — Hell, Len Corbett's horse! I'd better go and look for the darned thing!'

'We'll come with you — ' Lefty started to say, but Brock cut him short.

'No you won't. Keep an eye on Lucy and see what she's up to. She might even get ideas about going to Medicine Point for a marshal after this business with Harry. I'll make this trip alone.'

Brock did not add that he was not interested really in what happened to Len Corbett's horse: he felt reasonably satisfied that the animal could not possibly release Corbett from his ropes way out in the desert, granting it even found him. No, Brock's real reason was that, for once in his arrogant bombastic life, he wanted to be alone, to make plans whereby he could make himself safe after his crime. Otherwise he would always be unsure — never certain but what Lucy in particular would find ways and means to bring him to justice, especially as she had so many witnesses.

In this thoughtful mood he changed into normal clothes, and then got his horse from the stables. He was on on his way, not caring particularly where he went. Perhaps it *might* be a good idea to see what sort of a job the boys had made of Len, and even perhaps recover the lost horse. No harm in making sure. But he did not know which trail the boys had taken.

For a moment he was at a loss, then he shrugged. It should not be particularly diffcult to pick up the trail in the sands: there was only one way to the desert, and the tracks had been made not so long before. So he kept going, first following the ordinary trail, until at length he came to a point where there was clear evidence of disturbance. Halting, he examined what lay before him. Three horse tracks leading into the waste. He went on again, following the traces carefully, going ever further into the desert.

Now and again he paused and looked around him. The heat here was overpowering, full in the eye of the afternoon sun — and yet there was no sign of Len's body.

'How far did they take him?' Brock muttered, spurring his sweating horse into action again.

He went on once more, shading his eyes as he contemplated the shimmering waste ahead of him. And finally he came up against a surprise. The trail ended suddenly in a mass of hoof marks; there was a distinct three-track trail leading away from the disturbance

— but there was no sign of Len, or the horses.

Grim-faced, Brock dismounted and examined the spot more thoroughly. In fury he snatched up several ends of rope, obviously cut, and examined them intently. Then he threw them down.

'Fools!' he whispered. 'Damned, idiotic fools! He got away — and now he might be anywheres.'

He turned slowly, surveying the heat-drenched desolation, but nothing stirred. What had happened to the renegade horse he did not know, or particularly, care. The one thing obsessing him was that Len was free.

'I should have gone through with the hanging,' he told himself bitterly. 'Now I just don't know *what's* happened!'

Finally he returned to his horse, remounted, and slowly turned its head. His original reason for riding out here alone, so he could evolve plans, was almost forgotten. Corbett was free — and that meant anything could happen.

Lost in moody thoughts, Brock ambled his horse along slowly until he came to the more rugged portions of the desert which connected with the townward trail. Here, great dunes piled up on either hand, their tops misted with grains as the hot wind stirred . . . nor was the wind the only thing that stirred. To Brock's complete amazement something suddenly hurtled down from one of the dunes and bore him from the saddle to the ground. He had not a second to think before a terrific punch between the eyes knocked the senses out of him for the moment. There was a wrench and his guns vanished. Completely dazed, he stared upwards — into the merciless face of Len Corbett.

'I thought you'd be surprised,' Len commented tautly. 'I feel a darned sight safer with your guns in my hands, too. I took quite a chance attacking you without weapons. Thanks to you, I'm travelling light.'

Warily Brock got to his feet. He knew

he was on the receiving end of a showdown but his tough, earthy courage did not desert him for a moment.

'Thanks for my horse,' Len added drily.

'Y'mean it came back to you, wherever you were?'

'Not quite that. I saw a horse running wild in the desert so I gave the whistle I usually give to my own cayuse. To my surprise it responded to it, and you can imagine the rest.'

'I can't,' Brock said bluntly, his eyes on the guns. 'How did you happen onto me?'

'I saw you riding the desert, from my hide-out. I didn't know it was you until you branched off to investigate the place where your men had left me — then I kinda guessed it. I thanked my lucky stars for the horse and came to this point on the trail where you'd be bound to cross it. These big dunes make mighty handy shelter.'

'And now?' Brock questioned. 'Shoot the daylights outa me in revenge, I suppose?'

'Nope. That'd fix me for a murder charge and I don't aim to risk it. I'm just going to beat you up, for the way you've bounced Lucy Lee around.'

'I've never touched her — '

'Don't lie! I know exactly what you've done. and I want to give you a wedding present, too.'

'Wedding present? *What* wedding present?'

For answer, Brock took a blow on the chin that made him sit down in the sand. Len grinned down at him and thrust the two guns in his belt.

'OK,' Brock muttered, fingering his jaw. 'If that's the sorta fun you want you can have it.'

'I mean to, and this time there aren't any of your precious cow-pokes around to help you.'

Brock scrambled to his feet. At the same time he lunged out with his right fist and got in a blow that sent Len staggering. Before he could recover, another smashing right-hander jerked his head and he collapsed on his back.

Brock grinned and dived on him, then he groaned as, at the identical moment, Len's feet shot up. They took Brock clean in the stomach, flinging him backwards, completely winded. It gave Len time to get up and before Brock could thoroughly recover, Len lashed out a right and then a left. The first blow split Brock's upper lip and the second hit his ear with such force it nearly broke the drum.

'That settled part of the account for Lucy,' Len panted. 'This is for a dozen other things — '

A smashing uppercut landed under Brock's jaw, wheeling him round dizzily. He kept on his feet, gathered his scattered wits, and managed to protect himself from the next punch, delivering one himself. Len gasped and fell sideways. He only just kept his feet as yet another blow smashed on his nose — then another to his right eye. For a second or two he could hardly see, and what vision there was was of Brock's snarling blood-smeared face.

With terrific effort Len fought back. For an instant Brock dropped his guard and was rewarded by a bone-splintering punch on the jaw that rocked him on his heels. Like a tornado, Len was after him, delivering blow after blow. A final one hit Brock in the mouth. He dropped to his knees, to flatten entirely at a down-swinging punch on the back of his neck. His senses reeling, he lay in the sand.

'Guess that'll do for now.' Len stepped back, his shirt nearly in rags and sweat pouring from him. 'Next time I see you you'll get an even bigger dose.'

With that, Len turned and went over the dune from which he had originally leapt. He left behind a man nearly senseless and smouldering wth rage. Very slowly he got to his feet, crawled across to his horse, and with considerable effort climbed into the saddle. Thereafter the animal jog-trotted its way back to Ransom's Bend, its rider hardly caring what he did.

By the time the town had been

reached, however, Brock had recovered somewhat, even though he could hardly move his face and his top lip felt as though it were in plaster-of-Paris. To his chagrin, several of the boys were still hanging about the main street when he entered it, and they could not help but see him.

'For the luv of Mike, look at the boss!' Lefty ejaculated.

'Say, boss, what happened?'

In a moment or two, as he climbed like an old man from the saddle, Brock found himself surrounded. He was not slow to note that some of the boys were grinning too.

'All right, *look*, and get it over with!' Brock snapped. 'For your information, this is the work of Len Corbett.'

'But, boss, we left him good and hog-tied — '

'I don't know how you left him, but he's free and fighting mad. You couldn't have better proof 'n this, could you?'

'I'm more 'n surprised he didn't kill you,' Lefty reflected.

'Aw, shut up.'

Brock had been lurching down the main street whilst talking, his horse beside him. Then suddenly he stopped and asked a question.

'What happened to my wife? Where's she gone?'

'She went back to her room in Ma Cranby's and ain't come out.' Lefty jerked his head. 'We've bin watchin', like you said.'

Brock nodded. 'And what about Harry? Take the body to his house?'

'Done more than that,' a deputy replied. 'We had the doc come and look at him and issue a death certificate. We spun him a yarn. With so many witnesses there weren't much else he could do.'

'OK,' Brock growled, 'I'd better go and get cleaned up.'

With that he stabled his horse and then entered the Cactus Hotel. The quiet desertion of the wedding suite, which he had booked specially for the occasion, made his face set hard; then, muttering to himself, he turned to the task of patching himself up. Half an hour later he emerged again, tidied up, the only traces of his violent encounter being the gash on his lip and numerous pieces of sticking plaster. In a grim mood he marched across to Ma Cranby's and hammered on the front door. After a moment or two Ma Cranby appeared and looked at Brock rather doubtfully.

'Where's my wife?' he demanded.

'If you mean Lucy — '

''Course I mean Lucy! Where is she?'

'Upstairs in her room. I understood you were going to the Cactus Hotel — '

'We are!' Brock snapped, striding into the hall. 'After I've had a word or two with that obstinate girl.'

He took the stairs two at a time and would have swept right into Lucy's room had the door not been locked. Impatiently he hammered on the panels.

'Open up, Lucy! You can't stay in there forever!'

No answer. Brock swore under his

breath, waited a second or two, then brought the heel of his heavy boot down on the door latch. In a moment the screws were ripped out and the door swung wide.

'Don't trouble to knock twice, do you?' Lucy asked coldly, hugging a robe about her lightly clad form. 'I was just changing — '

'What *is* this?' Brock demanded, striding in. 'Just changing! Have you forgotten I'm your husband now?'

'No, I've not forgotten. It's something I'll *never* forget — but though I've got your name it doesn't mean anything more than that, Caleb. I — '

'You'll behave as a wife should — or else. Hurry up and finish dressing. We're going to the Cactus Hotel, to behave like a proper married couple.'

Lucy moved rather aimlessly to gather up some clothes from the bed.

'What happened to your face?' she asked drily. 'Or shouldn't I ask?'

'My face got like this because of Len Corbett. I had to teach him a lesson.'

Lucy started, and a sudden brightness swept into her face.

'Did you say *Len*? Then he isn't dead out in the desert like you planned?'

'He got away,' Brock retorted. 'I haven't yet decided what I'm going to do to finish him, but I'll get him in the end. It won't do you any good because he's alive, Lucy, even if you *do* love him.'

The girl quietened, thinking swiftly. She put on her dress, folded away her wedding attire, then set about brushing her hair. Brock watched her, one eyebrow raised.

'Taken you a long time to change, hasn't it?' he asked. 'It's hours since you walked out on the wedding party.'

'I've been doing a lot of thinking.' Her manner was oddly changed, and much more conciliatory. 'Just how much money have you, Caleb?'

'Enough for us to be all right. Why?'

'Oh, nothing. You're going to need plenty to keep your wife looking as she ought to look, that's all. Mrs Caleb Brock must be streets ahead of every other woman in town.'

''Course she must.' Brock grinned approvingly, though he was inwardly surprised at the girl's change in manner. 'And I'm just a bit puzzled.'

'Oh?' Lucy combed her hair carefully. 'About what?'

'You've done an about-face — and that usually means you're up to something. Mebbe with reason. You must still be thinking about the way that I crowned poor Harry — '

'Oh, that wasn't intentional. Anybody could see that.'

Brock moved slowly forward and took Lucy's shoulders in a steel grip. He forced her round to face him.

'You're on the level?' he demanded.

'Naturally.'

'And what about Len Corbett? You still love him, I reckon?'

'Yes,' Lucy admitted frankly. 'Still, lots of people love somebody else. It's a matter of obligation. I'm your wife now, Caleb, and that makes a lot of differ-ence. I want to behave *as* your wife. I want to make the morons of this town sit up and take notice. I'm no longer your hostess. I'm a sort of second-in-command.'

'Atta girl!' Brock grinned, wincing as he stretched his top lip. 'Keep up that spirit and you'll have nothin' to worry about.'

'*But,*' Lucy persisted, pointing the hairbrush, 'I want all the money possible to behave as I should, and to keep me quiet — about this and that.'

Brock nodded grimly. 'I get it! Blackmail!'

'Call it what you like, but money I must have.'

'You'll get it. I'm just thinking . . . the saloon pays well enough, but the real money's in other things.'

'Like cattle deals, for instance?'

'Yeah. I'm not hiding it from you. Like cattle deals.'

Lucy shrugged. 'OK, if more money's wanted, then steal some more cattle. Now I'm ready for the Cactus Hotel.'

7

It was towards noon on the following day that Len, lounging but watchful outside his mountain hide-out, caught the sound of heavy boots advancing along the narrow rimrock to his sanctuary. Immediately he was alert, snatching one of his borrowed guns from his belt. He knew the approach had not been made from the desert side because he had had it under observation all the time. It might be Saddles, but it might be anybody.

It was Saddles, trail dusty and sweating, leading his horse. Behind him came a tall man, wearing the badge of a marshal.

'Howdy,' Saddles grected, leading his horse to the narrow space. 'I made it.'

'Yeah — so I see.' Len put his gun away and looked at the marshal as he also led his horse forward.

'This is Captain Brand,' Saddles went on. 'You asked for a marshal, and you got one.'

Brand nodded, but he did not shake Len's extended hand. He looked at him gravely from his great height.

'Saddles here has given me the details,' he said, 'and because I think he means what he says I've come along to see what I can do. But the pair of you are under tentative arrest, so I may as well warn you.'

'Arrest?' Len repeated, lowering his hand. 'For what?'

'You're both outlaws, and you're wanted for hold-ups over the past five years. No use trying to deny it, Corbett, because we have all the details at headquarters. We didn't know where to look for you, until Saddles stuck his chin out and walked into headquarters.'

Len's eyes strayed to Saddles, and he gave a shrug.

'Not only you two, but we're after the rest of your gang,' Brand went on. 'There's quite a few of them, and

Saddles tells me they're working for Caleb Brock and that they'll probably be in any forthcoming cattle deal.'

'Probably so,' Len admitted. 'But Brock himself may not be in the party. What do you do then?'

'Go and fetch him. We'll get the truth out of him.' Brand paused for a moment and then added, 'You've as good as sold yourself, Corbett. You're a wanted man.'

'I know it.' Len sat down on a rock spur and spread his hands. 'I want to get justice, to bring to book the man who murdered my wife and son, and there was no other way except by calling in the law, despite the risk to myself.'

'I'm satisfied on that. As for all the other facts about yourself, we got them out of Saddles at headquarters.'

'I couldn't help telling them, Len,' Saddles broke in. 'If I was to get a marshal, as you asked, I had to tell the truth. I did, even though it's got us into an unholy mess.'

'I don't care how much you know, Marshal, as long as you get Brock,' Len said. 'I've no murder charge hanging over me, anyways.'

Brand nodded. 'Not as far as I know. All right, we'll let it go at that. I'm here for as long as need be, waiting for the right moment to rope in the rest of your gang, and Brock too, I hope. In the meantime, I trust you not to make a getaway. I hardly think you will because you've too much at stake.'

'You can rely on it,' Len said seriously, getting up. 'I'd better show you the inside of the cave, then you can make your own arrangements.'

'I'll fix some chow,' Saddles said. 'The marshal and me can both do with it. I got some over at Medicine Point.'

After some fifteen minutes all three men were seated just inside the cave, food and coffee before them. Brand ate silently for awhile, looking about him; then presently he asked a question.

'Saddles said something about dynamiting both ends of the valley down there to stop any cattle getting through. That right?'

Len nodded. 'So nobody can make a break for it. I figured it would be a perfect trap.'

'No harm in it, provided you don't kill or injure anybody — otherwise you'll have that added to the charges against you. You're sure playing with fire, Corbett.'

'I don't care if I am. If I think it's necessary to blast these rocks I'll do it, and I don't give a darn if it kills anybody, or otherwise.'

The marshal looked grim. 'If I see there's risk of killing anybody I'll stop you. That's all there is to it.'

'Oh, for Pete's sake — ' Len began, but Brand cut him short.

'Take it easy, Corbett. I guess you've lived so long on the wrong side of the law you've forgotten what's right. You're not entitled to endanger life and limb, and I'll see that you don't. Let that be an end of it!'

Len subsided into exasperated silence.

Then presently Brand asked a question.

'How long do you think it will be before Brock makes a move?'

'No idea,' Len growled. 'Might be any night — might be months. I've no way of telling.'

'Have you made any arrangements with anybody to tip you off if a raid is contemplated?'

'Yes, but I don't think anything will come of it. I fixed it so that Lucy Lee, the girl I'm in love with, would let us know. Since she's been forced into marriage with Brock I don't think it's very likely.'

'I see.' Brand considered this. Then, 'Well, you never know. Women do queer things sometimes, and take the most outlandish risks. Whatever happens, I'm prepared for a long stay, and during that time — though you are both technically under arrest — we may as well be as good friends as possible. Agreed?'

Len and Saddles both nodded, though what they actually thought was another matter. Len, for his part, had never expected to bring down the power of the law on his head by sending for a marshal. Saddles, on the other hand, was full of chagrin that he had been forced to speak the truth. Perhaps, some way, he might be able to make it up to Len.

And in Ransom's Bend, Caleb Brock was lying low. He and Lucy had attended the funeral of Harry, and no comments had been passed, then the normal life of Ransom's Bend had resumed its course. Brock was in his usual place in the saloon, disgusted that events would not allow him to take a honeymoon, but he just did not dare step out of town for fear of what would happen. He knew full well that a moment's relaxation of his grip would probably prompt somebody to report that Harry's death was murder, and from that would stem a load of trouble.

The only bright spot on Brock's landscape was the fact that Lucy seemed to have come completely over to his side, agreeing with every one of his suggestions with a willingness that astonished him. Not for an instant did he suspect trickery. As his wife, Lucy had now ceased to be a hostess. Most of the time she was over at the ranch supervising its reconstruction and deciding how large she wanted the rooms. At least, Brock reflected, it kept her out of mischief.

A week passed. After the upsets and excitements of the abortive necktie party and the stormy wedding, the denizens of Ransom's Bend were starting to get bored. There was no thrill in seeing Brock and Lucy drifting around as man and wife. Something more was needed. But nothing came. There wasn't even a sign of Len Corbett up to some trick or other, and Brock — for reasons best known to himself — had said nothing more about a search party. Things really came to a head a fortnight later when Lefty, as head of the now depleted gang that had formerly worked with Len, demanded a showdown.

'When's something going to move, boss?' he questioned, nailing Brock in his office one night just after the saloon had opened.

'Move?' Brock looked at him dubiously. 'In what way?'

'Well, no offence meant, but me and the boys can't go on forever without money. We're not officially on your payroll so we don't get anythin'. We've waited a fortnight for you to do somethin' — anythin' so long as we work and git some cash — but nothing's happened.'

Brock said nothing. He lighted a cigar and chewed it pensively.

'Like Len Corbett for instance,' Lefty went on, latching his thumbs in his gunbelt. 'An' Saddles. You're not goin' to let them two critters get away with it, are you?'

'Matter of fact,' Brock said, 'I've been waitin' to see if they drifted into town — Len Corbett anyways. I thought he might try and see Lucy.'

Lefty sook his head slowly. 'Not Corbett. Not that he ain't sweet on her, but he ain't no fool neither. Now he knows you're her husband he'll leave her be. What I mean is: why don't we go and look for him?'

'After a fortnight, I don't think there'd be much point in doing it. He won't be hiding in the hills all this time, doing nothin'. He'll be far away, and Saddles with him, mebbe.'

'I thought perhaps — ' Lefty began, but Brock waved his cigar.

'Shut up; I'm thinking. I was just going to say that my wife's never stopped asking me for money since we got married. I'm not surprised at that — and if it's necessary I want her to have it — but it's about time I was drawin' some in. Mebbe it's time I got some more cattle together and auctioned 'em at Medicine Point.'

'You mean your wife suggested a snatch?'

'Why should she? She knows all

about it. Certainly I need money.'

'OK,' Lefty said promptly. 'Say when and where, and the rest's easy.'

'Remember the Maitland spread?' Brock grinned.

Lefty's expression changed. 'Sure I do, but you're not suggestin' we raid *that* again after what happened last time, are you?'

'No, nothing like that. It's a matter of location. The Maitland ranch is two miles from another ranch called the Black Coyote. It's owned by one Ebenezer Drew, and he's so old he should have bin playing a harp long ago. His wife's an invalid, and bedfast. Point is, he's deaf as a post, and his outfit isn't so bright either. There's not as much cattle as at the Maitland spread, but it's worth having. It's a job of quietness, with very little risk. I think I can trust you to organize that snatch.'

'Thanks,' Lefty grunted.

'Grab as many cattle as you can, and by a wide detour take them to my ranch and have the brands changed. When that's done, transfer them by night through Vulture's Pass.'

'OK,' Lefty growled. 'I know that routine backwards. Guess I'll get the boys together. The pay's the same as before?'

'Just the same. Fifty-fifty on whatever the final sale realizes.'

'Right! See you later, boss.'

Lefty went on his way, and Brock closed the saloon down as early as he could and headed for the Cactus Hotel. He found Lucy at her ease, munching candy and reading a magazine. Brock raised his eyebrows.

'That all you've got to do?'

'While you're out — yes. Soon as the ranch is finished I'll have more to interest me.'

'If you want a change, get moving. I'm going over to the ranch — what there is of it — right now.'

Lucy put down her magazine. 'At this hour? What for?'

'I've a little job on tonight, and I want to see it's done properly.'

226

'A little matter of cattle rustling, mebbe?' Lucy suggested.

'Yes, and I'm not apologizing. Get moving. Time's short.'

'I don't see why I need bother.' Lucy stretched languidly. 'It's very late, and I'm quite comfortable. You don't really *need* me, do you?'

'I just thought you'd like the change. OK, never mind. I'll be on my way.'

Brock turned to the door, then Lucy's rather plaintive voice called him back.

'Caleb you've forgotten something.'

'Huh? Not that I know of — ' He turned and realized that Lucy was holding out her arms towards him. Immediately he came back, his ugly face wreathed in smiles.

'So busy thinking about things that want doing that I forget all about my little Lucy,' he murmured, kissing her vigorously. 'And I'm doing all this for you.'

'Who's in charge?' Lucy asked, surrendering to his embrace.

'Lefty. He's pretty much of a bonehead but I think he'll make out all right.'

'And you're trusting him to do the entire job?' Lucy asked in surprise.

'Yeah. Who else can I get?'

'Yourself.'

Brock seated himself, frowning a little. The girl, freed from his embrace, appeared genuinely concerned.

'I don't trust Lefty,' she went on. 'Not that I think he'd try anything crooked as far as you are concerned, but he's such a pigeon-brain that he might easily gum up the whole works. You don't mean that you trust him to get the cattle to Medicine Point afterwards?'

Brock looked surprised. 'Know all the moves, don't you?'

'If you don't want me to know anything you shouldn't drink so much. It makes you talk. But forget that: I'm on your side and want to help you. *Is* Lefty going to run the whole thing?'

'I'd figured it that way.'

Lucy shook her head doubtfully. 'You're taking a terrible risk, Caleb, especially when the brands have been changed. What is there to stop Lefty doing a cattle deal on his own account, not necessarily at Medicine Point, but with some of his outlaw friends somewhere? I wouldn't put it past him.'

'Yeah.' Brock mused for a while. 'Maybe you're right at that.'

'Nothing to do with me,' Lucy said, picking up her magazine again. 'But if I were running the business I'd see it through for myself. One slip and you might be finished. What are you planning? To run the cattle through Vulture's Pass?'

'Yes. Tomorrow night. It's the quickest way. Brands will be changed by then.' Brock got to his feet. 'Maybe I should supervise things,' he said grimly. 'Thanks for the suggestion. I'll be on my way.'

Lucy watched him go; then slowly her look of contentment faded. Taking out her handkerchief she set to work to deliberately wipe her lips. This done, she moved decisively towards the bedroom.

★ ★ ★

Back in the foothills, a bored trio was nearing the end of their patience. Saddles was on lookout, and the marshal and Len were dozing within the depths of the cave. Saddles, for his part — and maybe because of his mature years — was content to accept things as they were, but even he wondered how long the state of quiescence would last as he watched and nodded by turns at his post, his eyes making infrequent surveys of the misty night-swathed desert below.

He was in the midst of one of his catnaps when he could have sworn he heard a voice calling him — a woman's voice, far away.

'Len! Saddles! Hey, there!'

Saddles opened his eyes abruptly, clutching his gun. He blinked, listened,

230

and peered into the gloom.

'Hey, there!'

This time he got the direction of the sound, and it set him moving quickly along the narrow ledge. Suddenly he had a view of the entire foothills below him and he could dimly discern the outlines of a solitary rider.

'*Len! Saddles!*' This time Saddles recognized the voice of Lucy Brock.

'Here!' he yelled back. 'Right here! Follow my voice! I'm not showing a light because it would be too much of a give away. Keep going, and I'll direct you.'

The girl evidently heard him for she began moving. Thanks to the constant directions Saddles gave her she found her way successfully and finally dismounted from her horse a few feet away from him. Quickly she tied the animal and then came hurrying over — attired now in divided skirt and thick woollen wind-cheater.

'Sure good to see you!' Saddles exclaimed, shaking her hand. 'I reckon it's Len you'll be wanting to see. This way.'

He led the way back along the narrow ledge, holding the girl's arm so she could not possibly slip. So presently they gained the cave.

'You've changed your hide-out,' Lucy exclaimed.

'Sure we have. Hey, Len, wake up! You've got a visitor.'

Len, and the marshal, stirred into wakefulness. Saddles dropped the sacking over the entrance way and lighted the kerosene lamp.

'Lucy!' Len cried, scrambling to his feet. 'Sure is good to see you again.'

'Listen, Len, this is urgent.' Lucy pulled free of his bearlike hug. 'I've no time to waste. Caleb is making a raid tonight — or rather Lefty and the boys are — and tomorrow night they're coming through Vulture's Pass here with the cattle. Caleb will be coming too. I arranged that.'

'Great!' Len rubbed his hands. 'At last the chance we've been waiting for

. . . oh, this is Captain Brand, a marshal from Medicine Point. He's waiting the same as I am for Brock to make a move.'

Lucy nodded a greeting and shook hands, then she resumed, 'I've led Caleb pretty well up the garden by pretending I agree with everything he does. He seems to have swallowed it whole, and I don't believe he suspects a thing, but if you want to catch him you'll have your chance tomorrow night.'

'We'll be ready and waiting,' Brand said resolutely. 'And thanks for the tip off, ma'am.'

'Surely you're not goin' to return to Brock now you've escaped from him?' Saddles asked in surprise.

'I must — otherwise he'll suspect something and probably call off the cattle rustling. No, I must go back, Saddles. I don't think he has any boys watching if I try to leave town: he seems pretty well sure that I'm all for him. Tonight, anyway, most of them will be in the raiding party.'

'Sure they'll come this way tomorrow?' Brand asked.

'Certain. That's why I took the risk of coming to tell you. Now I must go. I'm so glad you're still safe in spite of everything.'

Len accompanied her to the outside of the cave and kissed her. He held her hand tightly as she turned to go.

'I don't like the idea of your returning to that swine,' he muttered.

'Nor more than I do, but I have to do it otherwise all you've worked for may be lost. Perhaps it won't be long, Len, before we can get together again.'

Len sighed and reluctantly released her. He remained with her as far as her horse, then watched sombrely as she careered down the slope, to be presently lost in the night mists. He turned back into the cave despondently, to find Brand and Saddles talking urgently.

' . . . but I tell you it's the only way of making sure,' Saddles insisted.

'Dammit, what do you think I did it for?'

'You'll not light either of those fuses without darned good reason,' Brand snapped. 'That's a warning, and I mean it.'

'Anything wrong?' Len enquired, and the marshal glanced at him.

'I'm just warning Saddles that blowing up the canyon isn't in the cards. There'll be easier ways than that.'

'Perhaps,' Len said doubtfully. 'If Brock isn't stopped by something approaching an avalanche we may miss him after all.'

'Either way,' Brand said, 'leave it to me to give the orders.'

Len nodded and let the subject drop. Since nothing further could be done that night he returned to his interrupted slumbers, and after a brief spell of thought the marshal did likewise. Saddles wandered outside to complete his spell of sentry duty even though he felt there was no conceivable reason for it. As he sat musing, a look of resolve came to his face.

'Reckon I owe it to Len,' he muttered. 'Yeah, I sure do for saying so much at headquarters. The other alternative is to be roped in for several years, and I never did take kindly to being behind bars . . . '

★ ★ ★

The raid on Ebenezer Drew's ranch was a complete success, to Brock's satisfaction. Towards noon of the following day he arrived at his own ranch corrals to find the changing of the brands already in progress. The squeals of the cattle and the smoking brazier told their own story; yet fast though the men worked it was well into the middle of the afternoon before they had completed their task.

'Reckon that will do,' Brock commented, after he had finished his examination. 'You know what you have to do, Lefty?'

'Sure. Transfer them onto Medicine

Point tonight, through Vulture's Pass — no guns allowed and only whips to be used.'

'Right!' Brock acknowledged. 'I'll be there myself to see no mistakes are made. I'm leaving Lucy to handle the saloon whilst I'm away. Be here with your boys at sundown. It'll take us until night to get organized.'

Lefty nodded. 'We'll be here. Right now we're going back to Ransom's Bend for a clean up.'

For Brock the remainder of the afternoon was quiet. He too returned to town — after a survey of the ranchhouse to see how the rebuilding was shaping up — then as usual he took his place in the Lazy Gelding and saw half the night's business on its way. On this occasion Lucy was with him at his request, but towards sundown he jerked his head to her as she stood chatting with a nearby customer.

'Take over like I said,' Brock said. 'You'll be OK?'

'Absolutely,' Lucy nodded, with a

complacent smile.

Brock glanced around him. 'If anybody wants to know where I've gone, just say urgent business. That covers everything. I've got to be careful. As you know, Drew reported that theft of his cattle last night, and some of the too-smart boys might get suspicious. They're just waiting for that chance.'

'I'll fit myself to the circumstances,' Lucy promised, and then she absorbed the rough kiss Brock gave her without a sign of emotion.

Upon that he left the saloon, taking care not to join Lefty and his boys as they too presently departed. As far as possible, Brock was disavowing all connection with those working for him.

And in the hills, as the sun dipped into a sea of liquid gold and quickly foundered in the night, three men waited — tense, alert, their eyes fixed on the misty groundsheet which was the desert between them and Ransom's Bend.

'Can't be long now, anyhow,' Saddles

said, spitting lazily. 'Maybe we'd better break company? Ain't much sense in all three of us covering one spot. How's about one at the entrance to the pass, one in the middle, and one at the closing end?'

There was silence for a moment, then the tall marshal turned his head against the stars.

'Corbett and I will watch this entrance,' he said. 'You can go and cover the exit in case they make a dash for it. And don't use that dynamite!'

'OK,' Saddles murmured, grinning to himself in the darkness. 'Be seeing you.'

In a few moments the noise of his departure amidst the rocks had ceased. Time passed — a seemingly interminable time to the two watching men — then Len straightened up suddenly.

'Hear something?' he questioned sharply.

The marshal stood rigid, and after a moment he nodded briefly. He could detect it too, now — the lowing of cattle becoming gradually louder and, as the momentum passed, the crack of a whiplash added to the sound.

'They're headed this way, that's certain,' Len said, peering into the night. 'Mebbe we'll get a glimpse of them soon.'

He changed to a slightly higher vantage point, listening to the approaching noise, then suddenly he gave a cry and pointed.

'There they are, Brand! See 'em?'

'Yeah. Won't be long now.'

The light was anything but good with only the starshine, but the ground mist provided some reflection, and indeed it silhouetted the goings-on below. First a few, then a dozen or more cattle became visible, hurrying in various directions until a cowpoke rode out of the murk and with a slash of the whip drove the beasts back on course — and the course was inevitably Vulture's Pass. Also by degrees the full complement of men became visible, some hurrying ahead into the pass, others to sides and rear of the snorting beasts.

'Quite a few men to deal with,' Len remarked, his eyes watching intently. 'Don't you think we'd better use that dynamite?'

'No I don't! I've a respect for the law!'

Silence again, so far as Brand and Len were concerned. They watched the whirling phalanx of beasts as the first of them came racing into the pass with a yelling 'puncher at their head.

'Leave 'em be!' shouted a voice. 'They'll go straight through here without you hustlin' them. Just see none of 'em turns back.'

'That's Brock!' Len exclaimed. 'Yes, there he is! The big fellow in the black hat, on the side there.'

'OK,' the marshal said, but still took no action.

Len fumed silently. He surveyed the string of beasts slowly covering the valley floor and heading out towards the further end. To the rear, men were still coming. Then at last, when men and beasts were all within the confines of the valley, Brand gave a shout.

'Stop there, every one of you! And stop the cattle, too!'

Immediately there was a milling of horses, a general sense of confusion, but nevertheless the movement of the steers ceased. By degrees the horsemen turned to where the voice had come from.

'Who's giving orders around here?' shouted the voice of Brock. 'If it's you, Len Corbett, you're out of luck. There's nothing wrong in transferring cattle to auction, is there?'

'Not if they're your own cattle,' Brand answered. 'These happen to be stolen. This is Captain Brand speaking. I'm a marshal, from Medicine Point.'

Down below, Brock started and looked at his men. Lefty was beside him, staring upwards stupidly.

'So help me, I don't know how this has happened,' he said. 'We don't know how many men the marshal's got with him, either.'

'OK, don't panic,' Brock growled.

'We haven't done yet . . . ' He raised his voice. 'Well, what do you want us to do? There are no stolen cattle here. You can come and examine the brands if you want.'

'I'm not interested. I know they're stolen, and that by now you have changed the brand. I've other reasons for wanting you, Caleb Brock, and those men with you. I'll come down and explain them, and one move from any of you will be your last. The valley around here is filled with watching men.'

Brock looked about him and compressed his lips. The cattle were getting restive — and so for that matter was he.

'Stay here and keep me covered,' Brand murmured, turning to Len. 'I think we can do this thing by sheer bluff. Brock doesn't know but what he's trapped on every side. I'm going down to talk to him.'

Len nodded. But Brock was not feeling in the mood for conversation. He was too conscious of the fact that he had fallen into a trap.

'Let's go!' he said abruptly, in the silence which followed whilst Brand descended the slope. 'I don't like this. It's neck or nothing, I guess. We don't know if the valley is riddled with watchers, or otherwise, but we're going to find out. Once in the open desert we'll find it out if we have to — *Right*!' He yelled, so his voice would reach to the further end of the cattle. 'On your way! Drive 'em through!'

Several things happened at once. At Brock's shout, the marshal fired into the air as a warning. At the same moment Len's borrowed gun spat from overhead. Brock started moving fast with Lefty right behind him. The rest of the men also burst into life, swinging their whips and forcing the cattle forward. And with the moments Brock gained added confidence from the fact that there was no volley of shots, such as he had been expecting — only the snap of the guns of Len and Brand.

'It's a bluff!' he yelled to Lefty.

'There ain't no more than two of 'em! Keep going! I'm going to get that blasted marshal.'

Lefty went on ahead. Brock swung back, pinpointing the flash of gunfire which, from its position low on the slopes, belonged to Brand. He fired, and it missed the marshal by several feet . . . then it seemed as though all hell broke loose.

Ahead of the line of cattle, as they were converging on the exit of the valley, there was a sudden flash of flame high up, the muttering growl of a deep explosion, and then the cliff face went flying outwards taking the rimrock with it. Thousands of tons of rock hurtled into the air and began crashing downwards in an avalanche.

Brock stared in amazement, watching the foremost beasts and men being obliterated under the deluge. Dust rose in clouds, and to the initial explosion there was added the genuine avalanche which followed it. Boulders and peaks from the upper levels shook, quivered, and then dislodged themselves as their underpinnings were torn away. Tons of rock, stone, and earth came slithering down in one enormous roar of sound, blanketing everything in a fog of debris, dust, and flying chippings.

Brand, realizing what had happened, seized the intervening moments to race down the remainder of the slope. He stopped at the bottom, his gun ready, peering into the haze and cursing the maddened beasts and general confusion. He had completely lost track of the men upon which he had been depending.

Suddenly there were racing footsteps in the gloom. Brand glanced back up just as Len Corbett came racing down.

'They can't get out!' he cried. 'I saw that from high up. The way's blocked by a landslide nearly forty feet high! They'll have to come back this way.'

Brand swore. 'I told that idiot Saddles not to blast unless I told him! He's killed God knows how many men. There'll be the very devil to pay for this — '

'Right there will!' A figure came out

of the gloom, both guns levelled. 'Drop your guns — and quick!'

It was Brock who stood there in the starlight. Furious at being caught off-guard, Brand dropped his guns and Len did likewise.

'Thanks for talking so loud,' Brock sneered. 'Saved me having to find you.'

He came up, then paused a yard away. 'Half the cattle gone and six men killed — mebbe more,' he said bitterly. 'Marshal, did you say? You're a darned sight worse than any killer, or don't you know the law? You've sure got no case against me. I've got an even bigger one against you!'

'The explosion had nothing to do with me,' Brand retorted. 'And you're under arrest, Brock, for the — '

'Don't make me laugh! It's the one with guns who does the talking, and just in case you've any wrong ideas on that I'll correct them right now. I'm going to finish you, and Len Corbett, for good. Then maybe we'll get a bit of peace — '

Brock stopped abruptly, a terrific explosion startling him. It came from somewhere overhead. Instinctively he glanced up to see what was apparently the whole cliff face dropping towards him. Len and the marshal did not try to gain the advantage: they ran like the devil away from the wall of rock which was hurtling down towards them.

Brock looked up for no more than five seconds, trying to fathom this second explosion, then he too grasped the danger. He turned to run, but those wasted seconds had lost him the advantage and he was suddenly over-whelmed by monstrous boulders that flattened him to the ground. Still others smashed down on top of him . . . and still more. Until —

Brand and Len ceased to run at last, conscious of the fact that they were clear of the danger. Gradually the concussions ceased. They looked about them and beheld what was left of the disorganized cattle, running aimlessly in all directions, quite unable to break free of the valley. Of cow-punchers there seemed to be no sign. Everything seemed to have disappeared under the rocks which had cascaded down from the heights.

'I reckon this isn't according to plan,' Len said finally.

'No.' The marshal's face was grim. 'Better look around and see what we can find.'

They began moving amidst the drifting, frightened cattle. Here and there they came across evidence. A leg projecting from the rubble: sometimes only a hand. More often than not there was no trace of anybody at all. Dead cattle were numerous. Finally they came to a man, face down under tumbled boulders. Len took one look, then turned away.

'You've been saved a job, Brand,' he said quietly.

Brand jerked up Brock's head and shoulders, then he lowered the body back again into the mass of boulders in which it had been trapped.

'About half the cattle gone, and every man wiped out,' the marshal said at last. 'I am compelled to add murder to Saddles' list of misdeeds. I told him *not* to.'

Len did not answer. He had turned away to examine something a little further up the slope. It turned out to be a man's hand projecting from the stones. A chubby hand. He was still looking at it when the marshal joined him.

'Another of the 'punchers?' he asked.

'No. This is Saddles' hand — I'd know it anywhere. The rest of him is below the debris. He must have been caught in the explosion himself. He fired the dynamite charges closing the exit — then whipped back to fire the second charge, which — incidentally — saved you from being shot by Brock. Me as well. But for that second avalanche we'd be dead by now.'

'Looks that way,' the marshal assented, pondering.

'I wonder if he meant to finish things

that way?' Len mused. 'Knowing he was under arrest when everything else was sewn up he may have chosen that way out. Whatever the answer, we'll never know it.'

Len turned away and wandered back down the slope. He suddenly became conscious of the fact that a lot of things had finished — his vigil to bring Brock to justice, for one thing.

'Well, I suppose that's all, isn't it?' he asked, as Brand came back to his side. 'We'll have to get these cattle together and return them to Ransom's Bend. That is, when we've smashed a way through the rocks. After that . . . '

'Let's clear a track,' the marshal interrupted.

He turned to the task and Len worked steadily beside him. It was tough going, even ghoulish at times where there was a shattered body to be removed, but they progressed steadily in reducing the height of the barrier. They had been at it for about half an hour when voices shouted to them from the top of the landslide.

'Hey there! Anybody around?'

The voice was not familiar, but Brand replied promptly enough.

'Yes, two of us. Come and give a hand.'

The man came down immediately, slipping and sliding. And not only him, but dozens of others. Even one or two women.

'From Ransom's Bend, I suppose?' Brand asked, eyeing them.

'Sure,' acknowledged the man who had first spoken. 'You shook the entire town with them explosions. What's bin goin' on?'

'Rustling,' Len answered, cutting the marshal short. 'Brock and some of the boys were driving the stolen cattle through here. There was dynamiting, and Brock was wiped out along with his men. Behind you you can see what remains of the cattle. The marshal and I were trying to make a way through.'

'Brock's dead?' the man repeated incredulously.

'Dead as he ever will be,' the marshal remarked drily.

'Say, that's the best news I've heard in months!' The man turned suddenly to the assembled men and women. 'Hear that, folks? Brock's dead! Reckon that solves a lot of problems.'

'Yeah — sure does.'

'What problems?' Brand asked sharply, and the man turned back to him again.

'You a marshal?'

'Certainly I am. I'm here to arrest Corbett. I was going to arrest Brock as well for cattle-stealing, but — '

'Cattle-stealing! That's the least of his crimes. He murdered his head barkeep not too long back in the presence of all of us, but we kept quiet about it for fear of the hell he'd raise if we did anything.'

'You mean Harry?' Len questioned.

'Yeah, sure. We figured out a plan to dry gulch him for that bit of work, but now it isn't necessary. Jumpin' snakes, Marshal, what are you arresting Corbett for?'

'Hold-ups,' Brand answered curtly.

'Then it's a darned shame. He's done more to put Brock on the spot than anybody living, and he tried to save Lucy Lee from marryin' the skunk. And that's his reward!'

'The law's the law, and I can't alter it. In fairness to Corbett, though, I will say that he had only one aim in everything he did — to get the chance to roam around and find the man who killed his wife and son. As a hold-up man he was free, loose and easy — could get around and have some money while he did it. It doesn't matter now if I tell you that Brock was the murderer, or so Corbett believed. He had the necessary evidence, but now it won't be wanted.'

'And you're arrestin' Corbett because of somethin' long dead and forgotten? Not even a murder charge against him?'

'No, but hold-ups are against the law and I've a job to do. Now let's get this barrier shifted.'

'Wait a minute!' A woman came from the midst of the crowd.

'Lucy!' Len cried in delight, as he recognized her.

'Hello, Len.' She moved over to his side. 'I've only just got here. Thought I might as well since the town seemed to have emptied. Well, I was right,' she said, glancing at Brand enquiringly.

'Yes.' He gave a grim look. 'Things didn't work out as I wanted them, but we stopped the stealing, anyhow. Now let's get a way made out of here.'

'Just a moment,' Lucy insisted. 'I've something to say.'

'Well?' Brand waited.

'You're determined to arrest Len Corbett?'

'I've no choice, I'm afraid.'

'Not even when the folks of Ransom's Bend want him as their new mayor?' Lucy glanced around her. 'That's right, isn't it?'

'Sure, we'll want a new mayor,' somebody said.

'Yeah, now we come to think of it, we shall. Somebody who can stay on the job and get results.'

'I guess few of us believed that you tried that Maitland snatch, Corbett. It was fixed by Brock.'

'It was,' Lucy said calmly. 'I know that: that was why I fixed it so Len could escape. Caleb himself boasted about it — privately, that is.'

Brock never had, as a matter of fact, but he was dead now and could not deny it.

'I married Caleb Brock because I was forced into it,' Lucy continued. 'When I knew it was inevitable I decided to play his own game and extract all the information I could from him. I learned something I had already suspected — that for the past five years he's been responsible for every major cattle-steal around here. Had things got far enough I would have passed that information on to somebody who could have made use of it. I couldn't do it myself because a wife can't testify against her husband . . . ' Lucy turned again to Brand. 'In face of all this, Marshal, and the fact that Ransom's Bend needs Len Corbett, you just can't arrest him.'

'What do you mean — can't? I shall.'

Lucy smiled a little and moved closer to Len. 'You have to have authority to arrest a person, Marshal. Right?'

Brand nodded, his face frowning in the starlight. 'Quite right. I have full authority to — '

'You haven't. The mark of a marshal is the badge on his shirt, otherwise he might be — anybody. Where's the proof that you *are* a marshal?'

Brand gave a start and then clapped a hand to his breast. He looked down at himself. Amidst the general confusion his badge had been ripped off.

'Look,' he said deliberately, 'you know perfectly well that I am a marshal. You saw my badge when you came to the foothills. Corbett knows I had one, too.'

'I've got a shocking memory,' Len grinned. 'All I know is that a marshal must have the badge of authority to arrest anybody. Otherwise he's a private citizen. True, you can get the authority by riding back to Medicine Point, but by the time you return lots of things might have happened.'

Brand looked about him slowly, then he relaxed. After a moment he spoke again.

'Whatever happens, Corbett, I've my job to do, even if I *do* have to ride back to headquarters.'

'The chance will never come again,' Len replied. 'You're checkmated, Brand, and you may as well admit it.'

The marshal clenched his fists as he saw the assembled people grinning at him; then suddenly he turned.

'Find your way out of this valley as best you can. I'm going for my horse. I've got to get back to Medicine Point . . .'

'You can't until these rocks are removed,' Len said calmly. 'It's the only way out. So you might as well stay and help us. Oh, let your hair down, man! You're beaten and you know it. The entire hold-up gang has been killed and there's only one left — me. By the time you get back I'll gather enough evidence to get myself free. There's nothing to stop you saying that the *entire* gang was obliterated.'

'I can't *do* that. It's against my principles.'

'At the moment you're an ordinary man, not a marshal. I'm asking you to see it in that light.'

Brand hesitated, then slowly his teak-like face broke into a smile.

'As an ordinary man,' he said slowly, 'I believe you're right! OK, let's get this barrier down. Come on, the lot of you!'

THE END

We do hope that you have enjoyed reading this large print book.

Did you know that all of our titles are available for purchase?

We publish a wide range of high quality large print books including:
Romances, Mysteries, Classics
General Fiction
Non Fiction and Westerns

Special interest titles available in large print are:
The Little Oxford Dictionary
Music Book, Song Book
Hymn Book, Service Book

Also available from us courtesy of Oxford University Press:
Young Readers' Dictionary
(large print edition)
Young Readers' Thesaurus
(large print edition)

For further information or a free brochure, please contact us at:
Ulverscroft Large Print Books Ltd.,
The Green, Bradgate Road, Anstey,
Leicester, LE7 7FU, England.
Tel: (00 44) **0116 236 4325**
Fax: (00 44) **0116 234 0205**

VENGEANCE
AT BITTERSWEET

Dale Graham

Always a loner, Largo reckoned it was the reason for his survival as a bounty hunter. But things change when he has to join forces with Colonel Sebastian Kyte in the hunt for a band of desperate killers. Kyte is not interested in financial rewards. So what is the old Confederate soldier's game? And how does a Kiowa medicine man's daughter figure in the final showdown at Bittersweet? Vengeance is sweet, but it comes with a heavy price tag.

DEVIL'S RANGE

Skeeter Dodds

Caleb Ross had agreed to join his old friend Tom Watson as a ranching partner in Ghost Creek, and arrives full of optimism. But he rides into big trouble. Tom has been gunned down by Jack Sweeney of the Rawl range, mentor in mayhem to Scott Rawl . . . Enraged, Caleb heads for the ranch seeking vengeance for Tom's murder. But, up against a crooked law force and formidable opposition, he'll have to be quick and clever if he's to survive . . .

THE COYOTE KIDS

David Bingley

When Billy Bartram met Della Rhodes, he was led to contact her brother, Sandy East, one of the Coyote Kids. Billy's determined vendetta against Long John Carrick — a veteran renegade and gang leader — made him an ally of the Coyote Kids. Carrick's boys were hounding them to grab some valued treasure, but only the Kids knew of its location. When Red Murdo, the other Kid became a casualty, Sandy and Billy had to fight for their very existence ... as well as for the treasure.

CALHOUN'S BOUNTY

I. J. Parnham

With his dying breath, a bullet-ridden man staggers into Stonewall's saloon clutching a gold bar, and names bounty hunter Denver Calhoun as his killer. Despite the dead man being one of the bank-raiding Flynn gang, the hunt is on for Denver. In Bluff Creek, when the unlikely Horace Turner wagers a gold bar in a poker game, Denver reckons that the Flynns are involved. Can he succeed in bringing them to justice though, now the bounty hunter has become the hunted?

HARD AS NAILS

Billy Hall

It was a trap. The knot in Tucker Flint's gut tightened at his desperate situation. Two more gunmen stepped out to face him — the odds now eight to one. Knowing death was imminent and unavoidable, he figured to take down as many with him as possible. His first four shots must be rapid, and — if he were lucky — there'd still be four remaining, whose guns would be sounding his death knell. Only a miracle could save him now . . .